PROJECT 17

LAURIE FARIA STOLARZ

HYPERION · NEW YORK

First Edition
3 5 7 9 10 8 6 4
This book is set in Garamond 3.
Library of Congress Cataloging-in-Publication Data on file.
ISBN-13: 978-0-7868-3856-1
ISBN-10: 0-7868-3856-6
Reinforced binding
Visit www.hyperionteens.com

ACKNOWLEDGMENTS

I had a lot of support and encouragement during the writing of this book, particularly on those nights when the story of Danvers State kept me awake. Thanks to family and friends who were there to listen, to encourage, and to cheer me on—you know who you are.

Sincere thanks to my stellar agent, Kathryn Green, for her generous guidance and faith in my ability. And a hearty thank-you goes to my editor, Jennifer Besser, for her keen insight, attention to detail, and contagious enthusiasm.

I owe much gratitude to Lara Zeises and Tea Benduhn, two amazing writers and friends who were there for me page-by-page, offering critical advice, time and patience, and a much appreciated sense of humor. Loving thanks to Ed, Mom, and Ryan—my biggest fans— whose friendship, love, and support are truly invaluable.

Thanks to Helen Jensen and to artist and author Michael Ramseur for answering numerous questions I had about Danvers State Hospital. A big thank-you to Mike Dijital, who was able to answer even my most technical of questions regarding all the little nooks and crevices of the DSH campus, and whose footage and photos made me feel like I was part of the crew. Thanks, also, to all who shared their DSH stories with me—those who worked at, lived at, passed by, visited, broke into, or simply knew of someone connected with the place. Thanks to Paul Sullivan who answered some of my filming questions.

And, lastly, a great big thank-you goes to my readers, who continue to e-mail and send me letters of support and enthusiasm—you guys are the absolute best.

—*L.F.S.*

We each went to Danvers State Hospital, the old abandoned asylum on the hill, with the intention of spending one night before the place got torn down.

Little did any of us know how haunting the experience would be.

Little did I know how the experience would change my life.

Forever.

—Derik LaPointe, filmmaker, *Project 17*

Danvers State Hospital

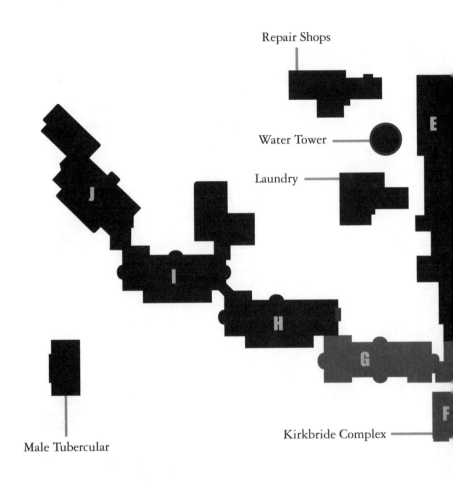

Repair Shops

Water Tower

Laundry

E

J

I

H

G

F

Male Tubercular

Kirkbride Complex

Male Nurses Home

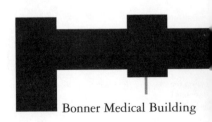

Bonner Medical Building

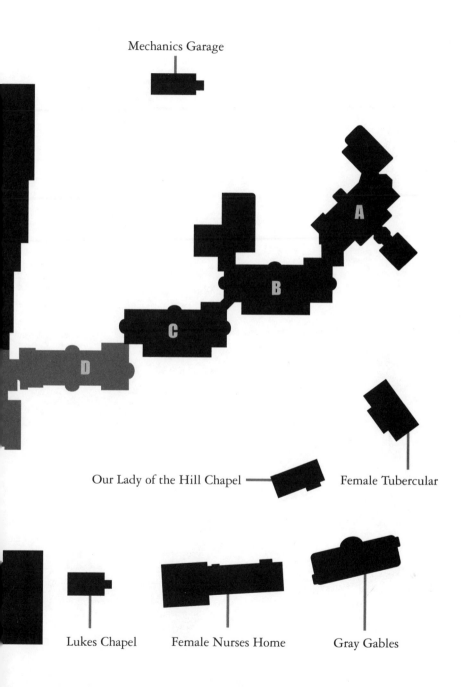

Mechanics Garage

A

B

C

D

Our Lady of the Hill Chapel

Female Tubercular

Lukes Chapel

Female Nurses Home

Gray Gables

DERIK

I TAKE THE ROAD that leads up the hill, my heart beating louder than the Cryptic Slaughter song that's thrashing out my car speakers. It's barely seven a.m. on a Monday, and while I should be on my way to the pit—a.k.a. school—I keep driving farther away from it, toward this place.

This abandoned mental hospital.

The idea of it, of how messed up this seems, almost makes me feel like maybe I should be one of them—one of them loonies who got locked up here; who got kicked out on their ass when the place closed down more than ten years ago; who now roams the streets trying to get back. Because this crazy place is the only thing they know.

Their home.

A screwed-up house of horrors.

I crank the volume, wondering why I'm feeling so unhinged. I mean, it's not like I haven't been here before.

It's not like me and my buddies haven't broken in on occasion for a late-night light-up and a couple or ten beers.

But for some reason everything's changed. Maybe it's because of the summer. I came here with this hot player girl and saw a bit of it through her eyes. The whole time, she was totally freaking—convinced the place was haunted, that we had to get out fast.

That something twisted was gonna happen to us if we didn't.

The speedometer on my dash reads fifteen mph when I should be going thirty. I all but stop before taking that last turn in, trying to calm myself down. I mean, what is wrong with me? Why can't I just get a grip?

I almost turn around, but then I remind myself of the alternative and decide that I don't feel like flipping burgers or scrambling eggs for the rest of my life.

And that this is a killer idea.

So I take the turn that leads up the drive. The front gate is open, and I'm able to drive right through—no guards, no fuss. But then as soon as I see the giant motherfucker, my heart starts pounding all over again.

A huge brick building with tons of pointed roofs and steeples. Big-ass wings that jet out at an angle from both sides of the main building—like one of Dracula's bats, like this is his goddamned castle. It's at the peak of a hill, which only makes it seem bigger. You can see for miles, all the way down I-95.

The place is surrounded by what used to be landscaped

gardens and paths, which makes it even more twisted, because just beyond the lawn is a cemetery, and in that cemetery rots a whole yardful of dead bodies. They're marked with numbers rather than names, for all the patients who croaked—all the crazies who were ditched and buried here.

Left like trash.

I heard about this one loony who crawled up into a heat duct to hide from the quack doctors, but only ended up frying himself when nobody could find him. I wonder if he's rotting here, too.

The trees that surround the place are the most twisted I've ever seen. The limbs are all entwined, like torsos and legs. Like couples getting freaky.

Or maybe they're getting smothered.

I focus in on this one tree and can almost make out a pair of eyes staring back at me, making me feel like I'm being watched. This guy from school swears that the last time he visited this place, some lady wearing bunny ears and painted-on whiskers—and not in a hot way—smacked her fists against his passenger side window. He rolled the window down to hear what she was yelling. "No more ice packs," she kept screaming over and over again. "Please don't give me the ice packs." Like they'd kept her in the goddamned freezer. And then she tried to get in his car, flashing him her set, like that was supposed to turn him on. The lady must have been at least fifty, the guy told me. *Heinous.*

Anyway, I doubt he was even telling the truth. I mean, supposedly this only happened last year, unless maybe she was one of them squatters who finally found her way back to home-sweet-creepy-home.

I try to look away, but I can't help staring back at those haunting tree-eyes, making sure they don't blink, that I'm not crazy, too. They stare back at me, almost like they want something now.

Like they want me to stay.

I look closer, tempted to get out of the car, to go up to them. I turn the volume down on my stereo and reach for the door handle.

At the same moment, someone smacks against my window. "Holy shit," I hear myself shout. I roll down my window, noticing the security officer.

"You scared the crap out of me," I tell him.

"What are you doing up here?" he asks—some forty-year-old bald guy peering into my car.

"Just checking stuff out," I say. "No big deal."

"You're not supposed to be up here," he says, picking at his yellow teeth like he just had breakfast.

"Why?" My heart's still beating fast. "I'm not doing anything wrong."

"This is private property. You're trespassing."

I hold myself back from giving him attitude. I mean, yeah, I know that I'm not technically supposed to be here. But it's not like it's at night. And it's not like I'm breaking in.

"The gate was open," I argue. "I just wanted to take a look."

The guy nods and adjusts his lame-o security officer cap. "Yeah, we're expecting a lot of people up here today—some construction people, some developers and surveyors."

"They're really gonna tear this place down?"

The guy nods and points toward a couple chapels, a giant medical building, and the crap-hole quarters that supposedly housed the nurses. "Just another week and two-thirds of this place will be nothing more than dust, rubble, and brick. They're gonna build condos and luxury apartments."

"Like anyone would want to live here."

"You'd be surprised," the guy tells me, still working something from between his teeth. "This place is famous. Been here since 1878 . . . even before my time." He lets out a goofy laugh. "Some say the lobotomy was perfected here." The guy jams his spit-covered finger into his tear duct and makes like a drill.

I nod. I've heard it before.

"You'd be better off coming next week," he continues when I don't laugh at his lame-ass joke. I mean, how is that funny? "Grab yourself a couple bricks, some stray patient files, and sell 'em on eBay. Don't think some of my own friends haven't already tried to reserve an arty-fact or two. I got a neighbor who has his eye on the main doors. . . . Wants to install them in his house."

"That's messed."

"Supply and demand is all it is. People will pay good money for this stuff."

I look toward the main doors, noticing how monstrous they seem, wondering what kind of twisted ass would want to install them in his house. I shake my head, completely surprised. But maybe I shouldn't be, because as crazy as it is that some people would want a piece of this place, or would want to make a home here—a place where patients were abused, where random bodies are supposedly buried, where screwed-up ideas of treatments were perfected—it's the place where I want to make my movie.

LIZA

IT'S TUESDAY MORNING, before first period, and I'm sitting in the guidance office, waiting for Mr. Trotter to finally open his door and let me in. I suspect he knows what this is about. I also suspect it's precisely the reason the door has remained closed.

"He should be with you in just a couple minutes," the guidance secretary tells me.

I nod and let out a deep breath, digging my fingernails into the fabric of my purse.

"Are you okay today, Liza?" the secretary asks me. "You look a little flushed."

"I'm fine," I say, unsurprised by my flushy appearance, especially since I feel like I'm going to be sick.

"Maybe you need a Munchkin." She tilts a box of sugar-coated lard balls toward me.

"No thanks," I say, managing a polite smile, wondering if they're pity lard balls. If she heard about what happened, too.

"Mr. Trotter is really busy this time of the year," she adds, popping a chocolate doughnut into her mouth and topping it off with a gulpful of some equally sugarfied coffee drink. I wonder if she knows how unhealthy her breakfast is, if maybe I should explain to her about saturated fats and hydrogenated oils.

I'm tempted to say something, but then Mr. Trotter finally opens his door. "Liza!" he announces, as though it's such a big surprise that I'm here, even though the secretary intercommed him ten full minutes ago. "Come on in, I was just on the phone." He opens the door wide, his normally shaggy dark hair shaved just shy of a buzz cut. That, coupled with his tight black T-shirt and dark khaki pants, makes him look like an Army recruiter—which, in turn, makes me wonder if maybe that's where I'll be headed next.

He takes a seat behind his desk and gestures for me to sit in the chair across from him. I do, noticing how my lips tense before I can even speak. "I'm sure you've heard," I say.

He nods, the corners of his mouth curling downward. "I'm sorry."

I bite my bottom lip, fighting the urge to burst out crying. I mean, he's supposed to be able to fix this. This is supposed to be some huge mistake. I half expected to come in here, show him my rejection letter, and watch in relief as he placed a couple of phone calls and made everything right.

"You just never know about these things," he

continues. "It's gotten beyond competitive out there. I'm just glad *I'm* not applying to college these days."

"No," I balk. "You told me. We talked about this."

"I'm sorry," he repeats. "But sometimes things just don't work out the way we plan."

"No," I repeat, shaking my head, refusing to buy into his counselor-speak. I can feel my face flash hot, the tears work their way into my eyes. "I kept up my end of the bargain. Why didn't you?"

"Hold on," he says, raising a hand up as though to stop me. "What bargain?"

"You told me you knew someone on the admissions board at Harvard. You told me that if I got all A's, that if I became this year's valedictorian, there was no way they could say no."

Trotter lets out a sigh. "Maybe I shouldn't have said all that, but I honestly thought that you *would* get in. This comes as a surprise to me, too."

"Did you call your friend on the admissions board?"

"Of course I did. But just because I can make a few phone calls . . . just because I can get an application a closer look by the powers that be doesn't mean I can get my students through the door."

My upper lip is trembling now. I push my hair off my face, noticing my reflection in the glass cabinet door behind him. My eyes are raw and puffy, and my normally pale cheeks look red and blotchy. "I worked so hard," I whisper.

"I know you did," he says, handing me a tissue. "But listen, it isn't like you won't get in to one of the other Ivies. You have other applications out there. And it's not like Harvard flat-out rejected you. Lots of people make it in from the waiting list."

"What could I have done differently?" I ask, wiping the run from my nose.

"Don't do that," he says, softening his voice like pressed powder. "Think about moving forward."

"I want to know," I insist. "You can say it. I can take it."

Mr. Trotter passes me another tissue. "Maybe some other time we can talk about it."

"Do *you* know? Did they tell you?"

He lets out another sigh. "It's what we talked about before. Your grades are flawless, no question. But as for your extracurricular activities . . ."

I nod, already knowing where he's going. "They're pitiful."

"They're nonexistent," he corrects. "I mean, I don't want to be the one to say I told you so, but—"

"You told me so." I say it for him.

"Look," he says, leaning across the stack of folders on his desk, "get yourself involved in something nonacademic."

"Like what?"

"Like volunteer work. The Ivies really love that kind of thing . . . a few hours a week helping out at a nursing home . . ."

"I'm having a hard enough time keeping my grades up

as it is. I don't think I could commit to something like that right now."

"Well then, how about debate? Or something athletic?"

"Debate scares me . . . and sports and I don't exactly mix—you should see me play field hockey. Not a pretty sight." Last year in gym class, I kept raising my stick too high, accidentally tripping all my teammates.

"So what *do* you like?" He lets out a sigh.

"Studying . . . you know—biology, math, health studies, physics—"

"How about something artistic?" he asks, cutting me off.

"Does doodling on my book covers count?"

Trotter shakes his head. "I'm serious, here. Think team player. They want to see you engaged with your peers, working toward a common goal."

"That stuff is hard for me," I say, feeling myself get teary all over again. "I'm not the most social individual."

"You don't have to be social. You just have to participate; you need to contribute to the fabric of your school . . . show your team spirit." He punches the air for emphasis.

"What about stage crew?"

"For the drama department?"

I nod. "I could maybe help build stuff . . . decorate sets."

Trotter leans back in his seat, unconvinced by the idea.

"I'm not sure what they'd need right now, being so late in the year. *West Side Story* ended two weeks ago, but maybe Mr. Duncan might have some ideas."

I nod, knowing that I'm being difficult, that I'm acting like a spoiled brat. I absolutely hate this side of me. "I'm sorry," I say, trying to smile. "I'm not usually like this."

"Don't apologize, Liza. Just remember that you have options."

"I don't know. I mean, I've always just planned on going to Harvard. I haven't even told my parents yet."

"Don't you think you'll do great things wherever you go? Why not think of this as something positive? Think of it as an opportunity to figure out what you really want."

"I really want to go to Harvard. I mean, I had it all planned out. Harvard for pre-med, Stanford for med school. My parents have been putting tuition money away for me since birth. My mom helped me decorate my room with crimson and banners. She even bought me my first stethoscope."

"So your parents really want this."

I nod.

"Well, *that's* pressure."

"It's my life," I say, correcting him. I'm Elizabeth Blackwell Miller, for God's sake, named after the first American female doctor. "This is what I'm meant to do."

"This is what you're *meant* to do, or this is what you *want* to do?"

I feel my face scrunch, taken aback by the question. "This is all I've ever dreamed for myself."

He studies me a few moments, as though trying to figure things out—when it seems so clear to me. "Okay," he says finally. "Get involved in some team activity and then come see me. Maybe I can make another phone call . . . see if we can get you off that waiting list."

"For real?"

He nods.

"Oh my God, that would be amazing."

"But no promises, okay?"

"No promises," I say, suddenly feeling the proverbial weight float off my shoulders. I grab one last tissue and dash out of his office, making a point to smile extra wide at the guidance secretary, since I may not have been the most cordial before. I even take one of her sugarcoated lard ball offerings and eat it in front of her, surprised at how good it tastes.

DERIK

AFTER MY TRIP to the loony bin, I end up going in to
school late, muttering something to the school secretary
about having car trouble. It's not like it matters anyway. I
mean, it's senior year. My grades suck. And I'm not going
to college. People know this about me, my parents
included, which is why every day after school I find myself
elbow deep in tuna freakin' salad.

Today when I get to the diner, my mom's waiting
tables. It was her idea that I go full time here on the weekends and come in every day after school. I've been doing
food prep up the ass—*that* and working behind the grill,
learning how to do the books, and how to run the place.
She and my dad want me to take over the family business
one day. This grease bucket is three generations old, and
they'd sooner be found guilty of tax fraud than shame the
family and let this place go.

Lucky me.

I think my parents are actually happy about the suckage of my grades, that I have no prospects unless I find myself some sugar mama to take me away from all this burger grease. I'm their meal ticket, so to speak. It was either me or my brother, Paul, to keep this place going. But he's already three years through dental school. The guy's gonna be a freakin' dentist—like it wasn't enough that he's first generation college—so it doesn't take a rocket scientist to guess who the suckah is in this whole messed-up scenario.

"After the tuna," my dad hollers, "I'll show you how to make them blueberry scones." He's got this huge-ass grin on his face which only makes me feel worse. I know the old man's proud of this place, of the idea that one of his sons will be around to keep it going.

"I got a date tonight," I tell him, trying to get the image of that psycho security guy out of my head—of that stupid finger-drill joke of his. "I gotta leave early." It's not entirely a lie. I do have plans. I'm going to the gym and, let's face it, there's bound to be a decent helping of datable girls there.

"Who's the girl?"

"You don't know her," I say, sticking a glove-covered finger into the tuna for a taste. Way too much mayo—this crap is heinous. I add in a few squirts of horseradish mustard—my parents' secret ingredient—to see if that does the trick. But it only makes it worse.

"Everything okay?" my dad asks, noticing how I look like I'm gonna heave.

"Just freakin' dandy," I tell him.

"Why don't you go along. I'll finish up here."

"You sure?"

My dad nods, taking a good look at the tuna—a soupy white mess that reminds me of bird crap. He dips his finger in to take a taste. "Like shit," he says.

"Yeah," I laugh, passing him the jar of mustard.

He lets out a growl, mutters something in Canuck—something about me, brains, and a baby pea—and then shakes his head since this means he has to whip up a brand-new batch.

"Sorry, Dad."

He gives me a pat on the back and moves over to his special drawer that's reserved for old diner relics. He pulls out the sacred spatula—the one passed down by his grandfather, and then by his father; the same one he's gonna give to me on graduation day.

Joy.

"You'll get it right one of these days," he tells me, turning the spatula over and over in his hand. The stainless steel shines. My dad knows every nick on the thing—from the time it got stuck in a pop-up toaster (who's talking brains the size of a pea?), to the time my granddad bent the handle while using it to fix the overhead fan.

"It was hard for me in the beginning, too," my dad continues. "I screwed everything up. I'm not just talking tuna, either: menus, bills, grease fires, food prep. Wait'll I teach you how to make corton; you'll be beggin' me to go back to tuna then." (Note: corton = ugly pig-fat spread.)

"I don't know," I say. "Maybe this isn't for me."

"Nonsense," he says, forcing the spatula into my hand. I can see the glint in his eye—like he just rubbed off a hundred-dollar scratch ticket. "Looks good on you," he says.

"I don't know," I repeat.

"*I* know," he says. "Just give it time. You'll settle in to it. We all do."

"Thanks, Dad," I say, handing him back the spatula. Part of me wants to do this . . . for him, anyway. The guy's so goddamned proud.

"Hey, have fun tonight," he says with a wink. "Who is it, the redhead?"

"Which redhead?" I smile.

"That's my boy," he says. "Have fun while you can, because before you know it, it's all over." He motions to my mom.

"What?" she squawks, catching his drift—the woman's a mind reader.

Dad comes from behind the grill to grope her butt and nuzzle her neck. "Still feisty after all these years, aren't you, Barbie?"

My mom lets out a giggle and smacks his butt.

My mom's real name isn't Barbara—it's Janet—but my dad likes to call her Barbie because she used to look just like the doll. Everybody says so. To me, they just look like parents, my dad a much older version of me—dark hair, blue eyes, buff body (for a forty-something-year-old, that is). They've been sweethearts ever since high school, but their families knew each other even way before that. I've seen the pictures—the two of them at prom, graduation, holiday parties at my grandparents' houses—big-ass grins across their faces like they shared some wicked secret.

Instead of watching them fool around behind the counter—a regular occurrence despite the customers—I pull off my apron and head for the door, knowing that in their own way, they *have* made a good life together. And they expect no less from me. They expect me to graduate high school and accept my post behind the grill with the sacred spatula in hand. They want me to marry the girl next door. She'll wait tables like my mom. Together we'll pop out a few kids. They'll grow up. One will suck at school like me. And then the cycle will repeat itself.

But it's not going to happen. It *can't*. I can't let it. Which is why I took a trip to that mental hospital this morning. When I saw the headlines that it was going to be torn down, I thought it was the perfect idea—to make my movie, capture a bit of history, and win my ticket out of the burger business once and for all.

I've decided to enter a contest I saw recently on RTV, the Reality TV network. They're offering a summer internship to a soon-to-be high school grad interested in pursuing a career in the TV biz. The idea of it—of *me*—as one of them TV producer guys, driving around in my brand-new tricked-out Porsche, coming up with all these cool ideas for reality TV shows, with girls galore hangin' all over me—is too good to ignore.

If the summer gig goes well, who knows what can happen? Maybe they'll hire me full time. Maybe my parents will stop comparing me to my walks-on-water brother, Paul.

All I need to do to win myself the gig is get my hands on a video camera, find myself a full cast of characters, and get our asses in there for one night—and without security guards to screw it all up.

And I have less than one week to do it.

Easy, right?

Not easy. Probably not even possible. A long shot, to say the least. But as corny as it sounds, I believe there's a reason I saw that contest ad. There's a reason that girl brought me up there this summer—in the daylight, when I could really see everything, when I could see things through her eyes. And there's a reason I saw the headline that the place was going to be torn down for condos and apartments.

So I have to give it a try—at least so I can just say I tried something. Or else I'll be smellin' like tuna fish for the rest of my natural life.

MIMI

I HATE ART CLASS. But when I got shut out of music this term—because all of those classes are reserved for people who actually *have* musical talent—my adviser insisted that art is the elective someone like me should take.

Someone like me who likes to wear black clothes. And black boots. And dye my hair to match. Because I wear dark makeup. And carry around a camo duffel bag for my books. And have a faux diamond stud pierced through my lower lip.

It obviously must mean that I enjoy stuff like art.

Yeah.

So while Ms. Pimbull, my art teacher—more commonly known as "the pit bull"—sits at the back of the room working on her grad-school stuff (an installation of watercolor hell: eleven paintings filled with nothing more than pastel dots and lines), we're all free to draw whatever we want.

I'm sketching a chicken head. It's got a hand gripped around its throat in a choke hold. It's not that I love or hate chickens. It's not that I'm some fanatical vegan trying to make a statement for PETA. And no, I'm not sketching out what happened during one of my moonlit rituals—as some of the administration imagine about me. (No joke. I once got called down to the principal's office, accused of vandalizing Winter Island beach with stuff like sacrificial dead fish and a giant pentagram made out of driftwood.) I'm just trying to piss people off—to feed what they already think they know about me.

When none of them have even stopped to really find out.

Derik *LaPlaya* LaPointe moves from his table across the room and plops down on the stool beside mine. "Hey there, Miss Sweet," he says. But he isn't talking to me. He's talking to the girl sitting across from me at my table. Nicole glances up at him but then resumes sketching a portrait of her boyfriend. She's got his junior year picture propped up in front of her for inspiration.

"Hey," she mutters, less than enthusiastic to talk to his sad self. She resumes her sketch.

"Is that Sean you're drawing?" he asks.

Nicole nods, all but ignoring him.

"How are you guys doing?"

"Great," she says, perking up slightly. She actually looks at him for two full seconds.

"I missed you at Maria's party last Thursday night," he

says. "It was awesome. I guess her mom kicked out that boozer-ass of a boyfriend she had and then took off for some weeklong retreat thing. The place was packed. How come you didn't go?"

"I had to study."

"Come on, a brainiac like you? Haven't you heard, the weekend starts at three on Thursdays?"

"Which is why you're flunking out of school," I say, cutting in.

"Are you talking to *me*, Halloween?" Derik asks.

"If the point-zero-seven GPA fits."

"For your information, I have a better plan than school."

"Male prostitution?"

Derik turns his back to me and continues to badger Nicole. "I'm doing this film project," he explains. "I thought that maybe you and Sean might like to give me a hand."

"Why?" she asks.

"Why am I making a movie?"

"No, why would we want to help you?"

Derik's mouth falls open but nothing comes out. "What's with you?" he says after a few moments.

Nicole shrugs, but she doesn't answer.

"It's for this reality TV contest," he continues, not giving up.

The idea of it—of Derik LaPointe making anything other than a play for some girl surprises me. I take a second glance at him, noticing how jacked the boy is these days. He's got on this incredibly tight long-sleeved T-shirt that shows off the bulges in his chest and arms.

"I don't think so," Nicole says, grabbing a strand of her frizzy hair. She brings it up to cover her mouth.

"I haven't even told you all the details yet," Derik continues. "I'm filming it at the Danvers crazy hospital."

"On the hill?"

He nods.

"Then *definitely* count me out." She adds a twinkle to Sean's eye with a yellow pastel, only it makes him look jaundiced.

"Come on, it'll be fun. Maybe you can get Kelly to come."

"Kelly's not even talking to you. And she's barely talking to me."

"They won't let you up there to make a film," I say, butting in again. I grab a red pencil from the center of the table and use it to draw droplets of blood spurting out from the chicken's neck. "They don't even let people tour the place anymore."

"Are you still talking, Halloween?"

"You're such a jerk," Nicole says to him. She gets up and moves to another table.

Meanwhile, I turn completely toward Derik, watching as he lets out a sigh and runs his hand through his gelled-up brown hair. "She's right, you know," I say, before he can get up. "You *are* a jerk . . . and an idiot, too. Because everybody knows it's impossible to break into that place at night."

"I have my ways."

"Oh, yeah? So you know about all the added security at night? That after five they shut the grounds down completely? No last-minute peeks. No final good-byes. They even lock all the gates."

Derik readjusts himself on the stool, as though finally ready to listen.

"I hear there's been something like thirty arrests there in the last month alone," I say, resuming my drawing, shading in the black fingernails of the hand throttled around my chicken's neck. "Everybody wants one last look before the place gets torn down."

"How do you know all this?"

"Let's just say I have *my* ways, too. I also know how to get past all those security guards."

"Yeah," he says, looking me over. "I guess that kind of thing is right up your twisted alley."

"Fine, forget it," I say, pretending his lameness bothers me. "If you're going to be an ass, I won't help you."

Sheer cave-age. The guy is absolute putty in my palm. "Okay, sorry," he says, utterly predictable. "Forget I said that."

I shrug and turn toward him again. "I could tell you, too, you know . . . how to get in, I mean. But first you have to tell me about your film."

"Why?"

"Because you won't get into the place unless you do. You know my father is on the zoning board, don't you?"

Derik crinkles his brow, not grasping that last part about my dad. And why should he? It's not like the zoning board committee has anything to do with the security business at the asylum. Still, Derik doesn't argue, instead climbs farther into the web I've spun.

But it's not like everything I'm saying is a lie. It's true about the arrests for break-ins—but the number is more like ten or twelve for the month, rather than thirty. My father, who *is* on the zoning board, told me he heard they've been beefing up security at the place—but I have no idea if that means they shut it down at five on the money.

Regardless, Derik fills me in—tells me all about his idea for a film and how he wants to enter it into some contest.

"I still need to get a cast together," he continues. "I want to use people who are different—people who'll spark lots of drama."

"Look no further," I say, completely piqued by the idea.

"Seriously?"

"Why not?"

Derik's pale blue eyes grow wide. He looks around the room to see if anyone's listening, and then lowers his voice. "Are you free Friday night?"

"Sure," I say, matching his tone. I add a little shadow under the bulging eye of my chicken head. "Is that when you plan to film it?"

He nods. "So what's your real name, Halloween?"

"Mimi." I sigh, annoyed that he doesn't know it— since we've gone to school together for four years now— but unsurprised nonetheless.

"What kind of name is that?"

"It's short for Miriam."

He nods as if it finally clicks. "So you can seriously get us in?"

"Sure thing," I say, since I *do* know how to get in. Thanks to online maps and chat sites devoted to asylum spelunking and urban exploration, I know exactly where to park, what time to go, how to dress, and what to bring. I must have planned out the trip at least a hundred times inside my head. I've just never had the nerve to go through with it.

That haunted asylum is the one place I've purposely avoided—the same one I need to see once and for all.

DERIK

AFTER GETTING THAT first bite, all I can think about for the rest of the school day is who else I can get to be in my film. During math, I come up with a list of potential candidates, trying to pick people from different cliques, imagining a *Real World* kind of thing—the pretty girl, the angry-on-'roids guy, the religious freak, the tree-hugging naturalist chick. . . . But nobody else is biting—seriously, I think I've been rejected by at least two-thirds of the senior class.

I know I could make this a whole lot easier. I could totally ask my buddies to come along with me—any one of them would join me in a heartbeat. But I also know that none of them would take my project—or me—seriously. They wouldn't follow my direction. And they'd sure as hell be shit-faced before we even got inside.

I need people who are gonna help me win.

So, after an entire afternoon and evening spent trying

to master my dad's mystery meat loaf recipe without any luck—the guy actually uses pickles, eggs, and ketchup—I head over to my uncle's place. Because I'm not giving up.

My Uncle Peter's a rebel, so I kind of look up to him. He's my father's brother, and he basically said "screw you" to working in the greasy-fry business, and now he teaches video production at Lynn Tech and works as a wedding videographer on the side. Once when I was in middle school, he complimented me on my cinematic eye, said I did a good job taping my cousin's Communion.

"Come on in," he says, opening the door wide. "You smell like your dad's meat loaf."

"Thanks, scumbag."

"Don't mention it, buttwad."

Me and my uncle have a pretty cool relationship.

He plops down on the sofa and cracks open a beer, clicking the mute button on the ten o'clock news, wanting instead to hear all about the details of my film. And so I tell him—about the contest, about how the thought of working at the restaurant until I retire or win the lottery feels more like a prison sentence than a way of life, and how I have less than two weeks to pull this thing together.

Uncle Peter doesn't say much, just nods his head, taking it all in. He's wearing the Celtics T-shirt I bought him last season—that and a pair of torn-up jeans and a Red Sox cap, like any one of my buddies. He's only a couple years younger than my dad, and looks so much like him in some ways—same wavy dark hair, same light blue eyes, same squarish jaw—but he also couldn't look more different. My dad looks harder, duller, a lot more tired. I wonder if that's what working in the restaurant does to you.

"Well then, that settles it," Uncle Peter says finally. "You've gotta win this thing. No other way about it."

I nod, thinking about my basically nonexistent cast. "Can you help me?"

"You came to the right place." He gets up and leads me into his studio, where he's got all his equipment set up. We spend the next couple hours talking about digital video machines versus Hi8's. He shows me features I'll need to shoot my movie—stuff like image stabilization and a 12:1 optical zoom. Then he has me adjust the lighting for the studio as a test, and makes me explain the benefits of close-ups, point-of-view angles, and extreme long shots.

"When you first get there," he says, "you'll wanna get an extreme long shot of the place—so we can see how massive the bitch is."

"Right," I say, "and I'll want to save extreme close-ups for when people get totally freaked out."

"You're really good at this stuff, you know that?" he says, nodding at my lighting setup.

"Thanks."

"Don't thank me. Thank that eye of yours. You can teach technique, but you can't teach vision."

I smile, pumped that I got it right.

"Come back tomorrow," my uncle says. "It's getting

late. I don't want your dad to think you were kidnapped by a pack of beer-guzzling aliens." He cracks open another cold one. "This stuff is shit for you, you know."

I nod, smiling wider. It's just so weird—so weird because for once I got something right.

DERIK

IT'S WEDNESDAY AFTERNOON, last period of the day, and I'm preparing storyboards in the library for my movie. Mimi, a.k.a. Halloween, is helping me since it seems this is a free period for her, too. Plus, it doesn't hurt that she seems to know the hospital like the back of her spider-tattooed hand.

Normally I take off during freebies, but I need to get this done, and I've already told my parents that I'm gonna be late for my shift—that I need to stay after school today for extra help with math. My mother could see right through my BS. She even threatened to call my teacher to see if I was telling the truth. But I doubt she will—the diner's an absolute zoo on Wednesday afternoons. There isn't even time to take a whiz, never mind make a phone call.

"Do you know how many tunnels there are?" I ask, glancing at the Danvers State map.

"Lots," Mimi says, sketching out a long dark one. "All the buildings connect underground through tunnels."

I nod, remembering that I read that somewhere—how the workers used the tunnels to transport the patients between buildings, but sometimes patients snuck down into them on their own, looking for a way out, only to get lost underground. I heard about this one whack-off who got lost down there for over a week. When they finally found him, the dude was buck naked, huddled on the ground, and rocking back and forth, whispering shit—something about his dead sister Suzy and how she wanted him to play hide-and-seek with her.

"What else do you want me to sketch?" Mimi asks, snapping me back to reality.

I point toward the front of the main building. "I was thinking that one of the interior shots could be of all of us sitting in the reception room, just shootin' the shit, getting to know each other, getting to know all of our characters right from the get-go."

"But we're not going to *be* characters, right?" she asks, tugging at her black Halloween hair. "Isn't the whole idea of reality TV that we're supposed to be *ourselves*?"

"Well, yeah."

"So what's with all the planning? Don't you want your film to look natural?"

"Definitely, but I also wanna go in prepared—do the research, check out maps, make sure I get all the shots I want."

"I guess that makes sense," she admits.

"Planning it out ahead of time can help you think about stuff like mood," I continue, remembering everything my uncle taught me last night. "Like what kind of mood you want a particular scene to have. I mean, if I don't think about this stuff now, it's just gonna look like a bunch of kids playing around. Even reality shows plan stuff out. At least we're not going in with scripts."

Mimi nods, taking it in, making me feel like I actually know what I'm talking about. And maybe I do for once. Maybe I've got a good chunk of the movie already planned out in my head—what I want to happen, how I want the cast to look, and how I'm banking on everybody's fear. At first I actually considered staging some scary stuff, like pretending to have some of my equipment go shitty on me, or rigging a door to shut when no one's really expecting it. But then I decided that those things would be lame—they might even screw up my chances of winning. Plus, we're talkin' Danvers freakin' State here. I mean, how can anyone *not* get scared?

Together, me and Mimi make up a slew of storyboards—for footage in the basement, the A and J wings, and in the art therapy room. But then she gets all weird on me, scooting back in her chair and shoving the storyboards in my direction like she's got something serious stuck up her ass.

"What's with you?" I ask, pushing the storyboards back.

Mimi shakes her head and looks away, her face all saggy like she's totally freaked.

I try to hide my smile, but I can't help it. I mean, if someone like Mimi's scared, I can only imagine how creeped out everybody else is gonna get.

"I thought you were into this stuff," I say.

Mimi continues to avoid eye contact, picking at what's left of her black nail polish.

"You're not backing out on me, are you?" I ask.

She shrugs and continues to pick.

"Come on," I bitch. "You're all I've got so far. You can't bail on me now."

"I'm not bailing," she says, finally meeting my eye. "I *have* to go there. Before they tear it down. I have to see what it's like."

"Are you honestly saying you've never been there before?" I mean, *Halloween*, of all people?

She shakes her head. "Not yet."

"So how come you know so much about it?"

"What do you care?"

"Just asking," I say, sensing that I've hit a nerve.

"Well, I gotta go." She stands from the table and pushes the storyboards even closer to me—like she wants nothing more to do with them.

"You're still coming to the meeting tomorrow night, aren't you?" I ask.

"Don't worry," she says. "I'll be there. With gloves on." She grabs a pair of those fingerless mittens from her bag and puts them on over her lame-o spider tattoo. Then she takes her stuff and leaves, making me wonder why she's being all weird and mysterious. Making me realize that there's a lot more to Halloween than I thought.

GRETA

TONY JUST WON'T LET UP. He's sitting in Mr. Duncan's director's chair, ordering me around like he's Steven Spielberg. It's the last class of the day, a free period for Tony and me, and, considering our drama-rat status, Mr. Duncan doesn't mind that we hang out in the theater—since this is where we end up every day after school anyway, rehearsal or not.

"It could really be a good opportunity for us," Tony says.

He's talking about this independent film project that Derik LaPointe is trying to rope us into. In a nutshell, Derik wants to film a movie at the old abandoned mental hospital in Danvers.

In another nutshell, Tony is sexy as hell, but he can be unbelievably relentless at times. When he gets his mind wrapped around something—like the time he wanted us to audition for *American Idol* even though neither of us can sing, just so one of us could meet Simon, since Simon's got all the connections—the boy just doesn't give up.

"Just think how this could jump-start our careers," Tony says.

Like me, Tony is an actor. But, as the writing on his T-shirt says, what he really wants is to direct. He's forever telling Mr. Duncan just where to put his clipboard, his director's chair, his spotlights. I wouldn't be surprised if he's already got visions of taking over Derik's project as well.

"If Derik wins," Tony says, "his film will be shown on national TV. Just picture it: *us*, on RTV with millions of people watching. We'll be getting auditions left and right."

I smile, somewhat taken by the image. I mean, this could be so much bigger than just another high school production, than just another stint with the community theater.

"Yeah, but what about the whole cheese factor," I say, snapping to my senses. "I'm a *quality actress*. Not some reality TV bimbo."

"Of course, babycakes, you're the best. Nobody's arguing that for a second," Tony says, in an effort to soothe me. "But you also can't argue the merits of reality television. It's made a lot of careers."

"Ten seconds of fame, more like it."

"Well, that's ten more seconds than what we've got right now."

"Okay, fine," I say, rolling my eyes. "Let's say we agree to this gig. What do you think the chances are that Derik LaPlaya LaPointe is actually going to win?"

"No matter, sweet cheeks," Tony says with a shrug. "Because even if he doesn't win . . . his film is going to be viewed by *real* industry people—the same people we're trying to connect with. Even if the film's a flop, just think of that exposure. I mean, look at what happened to Elisabeth Hasselbeck."

"*Who?*"

"That chick from *Survivor*." Tony rolls his eyes. "The *Australian Outback*. I mean, maybe she didn't win, but she's now got a sweet spot on *The View*."

"Big whoop."

"It's a start," Tony says. "I mean, just think about it— maybe those industry people won't want Derik's film, but maybe they'll want us."

I pause a moment and look at his deep brown eyes, at his irresistibly crooked mouth, and the three o'clock scruff on his chin. "Do *you* want me?"

Tony smiles, taking my hand and pulling me onto his lap. "Do you even have to ask?"

"Have I ever told you how sexy you are when you're trying to convince me?" I purr into his ear and then kiss him full on the mouth. He tastes like mint. "So what does one wear to a mental hospital?"

"What else but a naughty nurse's outfit."

"Oh, really." I laugh. "Wouldn't you just love that?"

"I'm ready for my sponge bath."

"Well, don't forget your rubber ducky." I cup my hand around Tony's neck and kiss along the nape.

"We'll be walking red carpets before you can say Oscar," Tony whispers.

The clincher. I spit the gum from my mouth and go at him full force. We topple back in the director's chair, landing smack against the stage floor.

But soon we're interrupted.

"Excuse me?" a female voice says from just behind us.

Tony and I pause from smooching to look up at her— Liza Miller, Salem High's next valedictorian. She looks more perfect than usual. I mean, it's bad enough that she has supermodel strawberry blond hair without a trace of dark roots, that her boobs are Victoria's-Secret-catalogue worthy, and that she stands five feet ten with the tiniest waist I've ever seen. But today there's a beautiful desperation about her, a vulnerability in her eyes—the kind I try to capture whenever I'm doing a poignant scene.

"Sorry," she says. "I was just looking for Mr. Duncan."

"He's in class," I say, climbing free of Tony.

"Oh." More disappointment; she purses her lips and looks downward into her hands, making me want to file the gesture away in my improv box.

"Are you an actress?" I ask her. "I mean, I know you've never acted *here*, but—"

"No." Liza shakes her head. "But I was hoping to get involved in some way."

"It's March," Tony says, getting up. "Drama's over for the year."

"Isn't there *anything* I can do?" she pushes. "How about for next year? Isn't there any design stuff I could get a head start on? Isn't there some crew that does that sort of thing?"

"Mr. Duncan hasn't even decided what the production is for next year," Tony says.

Liza picks at her fingernails, refusing to budge. It completely weirds me out. I mean, I don't even think I've heard the girl speak during my four full years here. She's too busy studying.

"Hey, you know, if you're interested in acting," Tony continues, "Derik LaPointe is looking for people to star in his film."

My mouth drops open. I shoot Tony a menacing look—the one I reserve for my most villainous scenes. I mean, what is he thinking? I won't be upstaged by some blondie bookworm actress wannabe.

"Derik LaPointe?" she asks, piqued by the idea. Her eyebrows arch in curiosity.

"He might not need anybody else." I sigh.

"I don't know," Tony says, oblivious to my evil eye. "You should definitely ask."

"Will there be a lot of rehearsals?" Liza asks. "I'm pretty busy as it is with my studies and all, and I hear you guys practice a lot."

I open my mouth to tell her about all the hours

40

required for just one measly production—all the weekends eaten up by memorizing lines, and all the weeknights we slave here getting each scene just right—when I hear Tony say that this gig requires no rehearsals whatsoever, that it'll only take up one night of her life—this Friday—and that it's a great opportunity for all involved.

"Tony!" I snap. "She said she wanted to do *stage crew.* Maybe this isn't the right thing for her."

"No," she says. "This sounds perfect."

"Yeah, I think you'd be great," Tony says, sucking up. "You have a great face." He makes a box with his fingers as though filming her face, and then pulls his pocket organizer from inside his coat pocket—Mr. Ever Reliable—to retrieve Derik's phone number. He jots it down on a slip of paper for her.

"Thanks so much," she says. "You saved my life." At that, she turns on her heels and leaves, stage right.

"What's with the look?" Tony says, just now noticing my scowl.

"Drool much?" I ask him.

"Only drool for you, babealicious." He pulls me close and plants a big fat juicy one on my cheek. "She's got nothing over you."

More like eight sexy inches in all the right places, not to mention shampoo-model hair, flawless skin, and movie star looks. "I want to be alone," I say in my best Greta Garbo accent, pronouncing the word *want* like *vont.* (Note: Greta Garbo is my hero—the most beautiful, most talented, and most powerful actress of the twentieth century. It's true—and sad, if you ask me—that most people my age don't even know who she is. But that doesn't stop me from trying to clone myself into her.)

"Well, I *vont* YOU," Tony says, Greta-Garboing back, trying to make his voice all raspy and deep. He snuggles into my neck, tugs slightly at my curly (Garboesque) brown tresses, and then wraps his arms around my slightly larger-than-size-ten middle. "Nobody's as sexy as you," he whispers.

I'll have to admit, it does help to lift some of my stupid insecurities. After all, I'm the talented one, right? I'm the one who's been acting since she was a toddler, who got a part in a toilet paper commercial when she was only twenty-four months, who studied with Claude LeBoeuf in Woodstalk this past summer. Plus, let's face it, not all A-list actresses are supermodel gorgeous, right? *Right?*

Yeah, Greta, right.

DERIK

WE'RE GETTING TOGETHER tonight to plan things out. I told my parents that I'm meeting some people from school for a class project, so they really can't give me any crap— especially since I arranged to meet the crew here, at the diner, where I'd be taking my dinner break anyway.

At about five past seven everybody starts showing up—first Greta and Tony, these two drama rats from school, and then Mimi. At about 7:20, I really start to sweat it, checking myself in the door's glass reflection, making sure my pants aren't too baggy, that my shirt hangs just right, that my hair doesn't stick up too much.

Because I'm still expecting one more person.

Liza Miller.

The most incredible girl in school.

I first noticed her during our freshman year—standing on the curb, waiting for the bus, this long and twisty reddish-blond hair hanging down past her shoulders, reminding me of ribbon candy. I think she caught me gawking at her because she paused from her book to look up—right at me, standing barely five feet away.

I tried to smile, to think up something cool to say, but then I noticed the title of the book she was reading— something written in German or Dutch or I don't know what. But it was way over my head. And so I just stood there, sort of dumbstruck—literally—watching her watch me.

"Is there something wrong?" she asked, wiping her cheek like she had food on her face.

I shook my head, noticing how her sweater matched the color of her eyes—an electric shade of green. I tried to think up something smart to say about it, but then she moved away, back toward the bus circle, probably skeeved out.

But that wasn't the end of it.

The very next day I got the lowdown on her—how she's a complete and total brainiac, only interested in books; how she doesn't give anyone, save the ball-busting teachers, the time of day; and how she doesn't date. Period.

Normally I accept a challenge when I hear of one. But every time I got close to the girl—to try and talk to her— I totally froze up. I mean, what do you say to a girl who's got her face in a book every time you see her? Who sneaks her lunch into the library, instead of eating in the cafeteria, so she can squeeze in some extra study time? The girl who sits in the front row of every class she's ever been in, who raises her hand to answer every question, and who asks the teacher for extra work just so she can get ahead?

Crazy. But what's even *more* crazy is that *she* contacted *me* about this project. She came running up to me this morning at school, asking me if she could be in my film—no questions asked.

"Are you serious?" I asked, all but jumping up and down. "That would be amazing."

"Really?" Her brow crinkled up like it came as some big surprise that I'd let her on board.

"Amazing," I repeated, feeling like a complete and total cheese-ass as soon as the word came out. But honestly, what else *could* I say? I mean, the girl is complete eye candy—like RTV won't eat that up. I wouldn't mind eatin' it up either.

I signal to Mom that my group is here and then whip off my apron to join them in the corner booth.

"Are we it?" Tony asks, pulling out his day planner. "Just the four of us?"

I shake my head just as Liza comes in. And honestly, she couldn't look any cuter—tight black turtleneck, short wool skirt, tiny black glasses, and hair tied up in a messy ponytail, like a hot little schoolgirl.

Liza scoots in beside Mimi, and I do my best to focus, starting with the introductions. I thank them for coming, tell them how great this is going to be, and then we get right down to business. We talk about all the practical stuff first—where to meet, what to bring, and what to say to our parents since we're gonna be out all night.

"All night?" Greta squawks. "Why can't we just leave when you're done filming?"

"It won't take all night," Tony says to assure her. "A small-budget production like this shouldn't take us more than a few hours."

"No way," I say. "We're spending the night—end of story."

After all, there's a big difference between only having to stick it out for a couple hours, and knowing that you're stuck there all night—until the next morning.

"Why can't we just *pretend* to stay there all night?" Greta pushes. "We can totally make it look legit with some sleeping bags and backpacks."

"I want to do this right," I say. "If we play around, it's gonna look like we're *playing around*. I want this to be real."

"You're obviously not familiar with my acting abilities," Greta says with an eye roll. "I make things look real."

"*Realer* than real, babycakes." Tony winks at her.

"Wear dark clothes," I say, ignoring their crap. "And bring water and convenient stuff to eat—stuff you don't have to cook." I look at Liza, who's actually taking notes, writing down my every word like this is history class or something.

"Anything else?" she asks, peering up at me when she's finished writing.

I want to tell her yes—that I can't help but wonder if she remembers me from that day, freshman year, near the bus circle, when I couldn't stop gawking at her.

"We should carpool," Mimi says, snapping me back to the moment. "The place where we're going to park is pretty dead at night. It would suck if a cop drove by and saw a row of cars. It would definitely give us away."

"Is it true the place is haunted?" Greta asks, fidgeting with the salt and pepper shakers.

"Don't worry, babealicious, I'll be there to protect you." Tony—no bigger than my pinkie—wraps his matchstick arm around Greta, like the guy would even stand a chance saving himself from a baby kitten.

"What do you mean by *haunted*?" Liza cuts in.

"Are you serious?" Mimi laughs. "You haven't heard about all the weird stuff that's happened there? People say that it doesn't even matter what the temperature is outside—I mean, it could be a blazing-hot summer day but it's always super cold in there. They say you can hear the patients whispering through the drafts, telling you all about their suffering."

Liza's eyes get mother-big, making me want to put a muzzle on Mimi, since all I need right now is for someone to back out, let alone *Liza*.

"It's not illegal to go up there, is it?" Liza asks.

Mimi's stud-pierced lip drops open. "What, do you live under a rock?"

Luckily, my mother interrupts the moment. She

smacks a plateful of day-old lemon doughnuts onto the table. "You kids working hard?"

I nod and flash her a smile, thankful that she doesn't hang around.

A few moments later, the doorbells jangle as Chet pushes his way in. "Hey, scumbag," I say. "What are *you* doing here?" He's all wrapped up in some towel-like thing, like a straitjacket, so his arms and hands don't move. "What the hell are you doing?" I ask him.

"Dressing for the occasion," he jokes.

"Are you serious? You changed your mind?"

Chet was one of the first people I asked. Not because he's a good buddy of mine or anything. The guy's more annoying than anything else. He's a clown—he even looks a little like one, with his pasty white face and curly orange hair. But he *tries* to be funny, and, all considered, I thought the movie might need some of that.

"Yeah, I'm going," he says. "This mummy stuff is pretty hot."

"Who clocked you?" I ask, noticing his shiner—a dark patch right below his left eye.

"Nobody," he says. "I just thought it went with the outfit."

"You're the man," I say, standing up. Not thinking, I go to give him a high five, but instead, end up fiveing his elbow.

I pull a chair over for him, and we get back down to business, talking about our plans for another good half hour. "So tomorrow night," I say as things are breaking up.

I take one last look at my group—at Greta and Tony, now feeding each other fingerfuls of lemon filling from the doughnuts; at Liza, still taking notes; at Mimi in all her layers of blackness; and then at Chet in his straitjacket.

"This is gonna be one bitchin' movie," I say, more excited than I ever thought possible.

DERIK

AFTER THE MEETING at the diner, I head over to my uncle's apartment for one last video lesson. Except it turns out to be more like a final exam. Uncle Peter actually made up a test, including a written section, a visual part where I have to watch various movie clips and describe the shots they used and why, and a hands-on part where I have to go outside and shoot in his backyard. The guy's a whack, but I score an A—the only A I ever got . . . aside from gym, that is.

"You're really taking this thing seriously, aren't you?" he says, plunking down across from me at the kitchen table.

"I really wanna win."

"Have you told your parents yet?"

I shake my head and look away.

"I take it that's a no?"

"If I don't win, there's no need to tell 'em."

"Why not? It's *your* life. Contest or not, you've got some real talent with this. If you want to go for it, go for it; but don't let some contest dictate your life. You need to do what you want."

"Tell *them* that."

"*You* tell 'em."

I shrug again, knowing that I can't, that my parents are counting on me to continue the business; that even if I *do* win, I don't know what the hell I'm gonna do—how the hell I'm gonna break it to them.

"You know you're gonna need some kickin' equipment, don't you?" he says.

"Thanks, Uncle Pete," I say, hoping he's gonna loan me one of the digital cameras he reserves only for his senior class students.

He gets up and heads for his studio, coming back just a few seconds later and placing his Sony DV camcorder in my lap—the same one that cost him more than $3,000, the one he uses for wedding gigs. "Be gentle with her," he says. "She's an easy lover, but she's delicate just the same."

"Are you kidding me? I can't take *this*."

"You gotta take it. That girl gives the best film of any babe I've ever had. She's also got night vision—don't need to worry about working her in the dark. This babe's got it all."

"Are you kidding me?" I repeat.

"Take it," Uncle Peter says. "And take my dolly, a couple shotgun mics, and a bunch of DV tapes, too. The dolly will help keep you steady as you're shooting down those long corridors. Nothing worse for a filmmaker than a shaky hand."

"Wow, I don't know what to say. Thanks, man."

My uncle smiles, proud of me, I think. "Come by over the weekend, after the shoot," he says. "I can teach you a thing or two about editing your footage. I've got a new program that works the nuts."

"Thanks," I repeat, excited by his enthusiasm, by how good it feels to have somebody be proud of me for once.

CHET

TWO NIGHTS AGO my dad got so hammered that he ended up backhanding me across the face. He doesn't normally do that. Normally when he drinks, I just keep my bedroom door closed and locked. Normally I try to keep out of his way. But two nights ago I didn't.

My dad got pissed that my music was too loud, that I ate the last banana, drank the last Pepsi, didn't thank him for serving in Desert Storm. And so he smacked me—*hard*—making my eye socket feel like it was going to explode.

The guy just refuses to put the bottle down.

We haven't talked since it happened, so I'm not even sure if he remembers that he did it. But I wonder if he notices the shiner he left me with—if he asks himself where it came from. If he's even looked at me to check it out.

Suffice it to say, the idea of getting away for one night

is too tempting to ignore. And so here I am, driving to Danvers crazy hospital, wondering if maybe I should turn around and just camp out someplace in my car for the night. But maybe it won't be so bad. I mean, once you subtract the whole spending-the-night-in-a-haunted-asylum factor, there are definite benefits to this trip. For one, there are going to be girls there. For another, those same girls are going to be scared. And third, scared girls + hard-up Chet = possible nookie.

What's it been, like, a year since I had a date?

The truth is the asylum has always intrigued me— driving down Route 1, passing the local strip clubs, wishing I had a fake ID to actually get inside said local strip clubs. And then seeing the asylum peaks and steeples peeping up at the top of the hill. I remember the first time I saw it. I was at the mini-golf course in Middleton with some of my buds. All you saw ahead of you was this giant brick castle sprawled out in the distance at the top of a hill. I asked my friend what it was and he told me; only, he called it the witch's castle, claiming that the judge for the Salem witch trials used to live there—the guy who had all those people hung. Sometime after Judge Hathorne moved, they tore the house down and built the asylum. So it's almost as if, with a history like that, the place never stood a chance.

I drive down Route 62, noticing the hospital driveway on the left at the turnabout, but speeding past it. Mimi, who seems to know a little too much about the asylum if you ask me, says it's best to access the campus off the beaten path since cops are notorious for hanging around the entrance. So I take the exit for Route 1 South, remembering how Derik said that we should get to our meeting place between nine and nine thirty, rather than arriving all at once. It's a little after nine now, so I'm hoping I'm the first, hoping that maybe I can hide and then sneak up on Derik and the others and spook them all out, lighten the mood a bit, maybe—since I'm thinking they're going to need it.

I pull into the office park where we're supposed to meet, and drive around to the back of the buildings. The parking lot is mostly deserted except for a few cars, all empty—maybe a sparse night crew working at the electronics company. You can see the outline of the hospital from here—all the pointy steeples, like a creepy sort of church. There's a wooded hill that leads up to the place, but it's completely dark—like a horror movie about to happen.

I take a look at myself in the rearview mirror and try to calm myself down, to tame all my stupid cowlicks. Unfortunately, I inherited my father's curly orange hair. Unfortunately, I'm not exactly *GQ* material with my ghost-white face and freckly nose, and now the shiner I've got to top the picture off. But who knows, maybe one of these girls will have a soft spot (or two) for tall, banged-up, and funny.

Slicking my hair back as best I can with one hand, I

stretch my brain cap over the crown of my head with the other. It's one of those second-skin bathing caps. It's got a picture of a brain on the top, making me look like a bald man with a lobotomy. I wore it last year to a Halloween party and pulled it out for tonight (among other party pleasers) since, for obvious reasons, it suits the occasion well.

A few minutes later, I spot a car pulling into the lot. It's Derik's—a dark blue Chevy truck. He backs in a couple cars down from mine, but he doesn't get out—just kind of sits there with his headlights shut off, engine halted, like he doesn't even know I'm here.

I grab my backpack and scoot out quick, hoping he doesn't spot me. I can see the shadow of him sitting there. Mimi's in there, too, sitting in the passenger side. The lights in the parking lot are anything but bright, but I'm still able to make out her kinky black hair.

I walk as slowly and quietly as I can toward the driver's side. Then I smack my palms against the window and let out a sickly moan—the victim of a lobotomy. I even lower my head so they can see the brains.

"What the hell are you doing, man?" Derik shouts, rolling down the window.

"What?" I ask, the smile melting off my face. I look at Mimi to see if maybe she has a sense of humor, but she looks just as peeved.

"Are you trying to get us bagged before we even get up there?" Derik asks. "Get that thing off your head. You're supposed to be wearing black."

"I *am* wearing black," I argue, pulling a black knitted hat on over my brain cap.

Derik sighs and leans back in his seat, clearly stressed. He checks his watch. "Nine twenty," he whispers. "Where the hell is everybody?"

"Getting fitted for straitjackets," I joke.

But Derik doesn't appreciate my humor. "How 'bout I pop you in your other eye?" he says.

A few moments later, another car pulls into the lot. "This is probably them," Mimi says, pulling on a black ski mask. At first I think the mask is a joke—that she's on the same wavelength as me—but she doesn't even crack a smile.

Tony and Greta get out of their car, dudded out in black as well. Greta's got on a long black skirt with a black fur jacket that reminds me of Shithead, my cat.

"Are you gonna be able to climb in that outfit?" Derik asks her, stepping out of his truck.

"You said dark clothing," she says, in the deepest, huskiest voice I've ever heard come out of a girl. "And for your information, this skirt is Calvin Klein. As a film-maker, you should be grateful that I took so much time with my wardrobe."

"I'll be grateful if you can get your ass up that hill," Derik says.

"You look amazing," Tony tells her, giving her butt a good rap.

"Are you sure? I mean, maybe the fur is overkill. No

pun intended. I don't want those PETA people talking trash about me in some tabloid."

"Amazing," Tony chirps, a high-pitched voice like someone kicked him in the jewels. "Like a real A-lister."

Whatever that means, it totally perks Greta up. The girl snuggles up to his Slim Jim figure and purrs into his neck.

"Get a room," Mimi says.

"Preferably one with some shock equipment," I say. "Could add a real zap to the experience."

"Where's Liza?" Derik asks, ignoring my joke.

"She's with us," Greta says, pausing between purrs.

I look toward their car and notice a shadow moving in the backseat.

"Let's just say she's a tad bit nervous," Tony says.

"More like a basket case," Greta corrects. "This obviously wasn't a good idea for her."

Derik unzips his DV recorder from its case and turns it on.

"What are you doing?" I ask.

Instead of answering, he brings the recorder over to Tony's car. He knocks on the window, and Liza lets him in.

"That's really smart," Tony says, once Derik's inside. "Get the drama on film right from the get-go."

"Or the smut," I say, knowing full well about Derik's male-slut reputation (and envying it), wondering if Derik's trying at this very moment to capitalize on Liza's nerves. I mean, who would be that sketchy?

Um, I mean except for me.

A few minutes later, Liza comes out. Her arms are folded and there's a worried expression across her face, her lips pursed together like she's on her way to have root canal or something. I'm half tempted to pull off my hat so she can see my lobotomy cap, thinking that it'll make her laugh. "Are you all right?" I ask instead.

Liza nods, but her eyes are focused on the hill—on how steep it is, maybe, or how the trees and brush look so thick.

"She's been doing some online research about the place," Derik tells us. He pulls a hooded sweatshirt from his bag and drapes it around her shoulders, totally stealing my game.

"The Internet can be a dangerous place," I say. "I once got so obsessed with female wrestlers, I couldn't stop surfing for pics—girls in headlocks, giving each other noogies, doing body slams, pulling each other's hair." I close my eyes and smile for effect, as though lost in the Land of Reminisce. "After a while I couldn't sleep at night, couldn't get my mind to shut off."

"More like you couldn't get Mr. Righty to shut off," Mimi says, gesturing up and down with her hand.

"Funny that you would automatically think of Mr. Wanky at a time like this." I wink. "Anything you need to tell me . . . or show me?"

"Thanks for that image," Derik says.

But at least it makes Liza smile. And Mimi smiles too. I can see the corner of her mouth turn upward, even under that ski mask.

* * *

The wooded hill that leads up to the hospital is just behind us. Derik gives us each a walkie-talkie and a head-mounted flashlight.

"This could be kinky," I say, pulling the flashlight cap-thing over my head, so that the beam angles out from my forehead.

We work our way up and sideways along the hill, fighting through branch-and-brush hell the entire way. The forest is thicker than I'd expect for March. Everything's still dead from winter, but that also means my various body parts are icing up. It's so *effing* cold up here, I just want to curl into a tiny ball.

We keep moving forward at a decent clip, Mimi in the lead with Derik close behind her, his camera propped atop his shoulder, ever eager for fruity footage. I'm in the back, following behind Liza, ready to swoop in and give her a shoulder—or the body part of her choice—in case she needs it.

Nobody really says anything—not when we pass the first sign promising jail time and fines for all who trespass, and not when we pass the twentieth sign that promises the same thing. It seems we're already on hospital property. Apparently, according to Mimi—oh, wise one of haunted asylums—Danvers State spans five hundred acres of land. I press the SPEAK button on my walkie-talkie and let out a couple Jason-from-*Friday-the-13th* grunts, a couple *che-che-che-heh-heh-heh*'s to lighten the mood, but nobody seems to appreciate it.

"Are you *trying* to get us caught?" Derik's voice plays through my speaker.

"I'm *trying* to make this interesting," I argue, wondering if everybody's sense of humor got extracted with the last lobotomy. At the same moment, a sharp branch scratches across my chin. "Crap!"

"Are you all right?" Liza asks, peeking back at me.

"Better now," I say, happy for her concern. Even happier that she's walking right in front of me, where I can score a good view of her lucky (for me) Seven jeans.

A good twenty minutes—and eighty scratches later—and we finally make it up to the top. Derik, still filming, orders us to click off our headlights to avoid being seen, and then we sprint across what appears to be a meadow of sorts.

Until we finally get there. And see it. It's like a huge rush, and I have no idea why. I have no idea why I even care. I mean, the place is creepy to the fiftieth power. There are a couple of spotlights strategically placed about the grounds—for the patrol guys, no doubt—enabling us to get a decent view. The main building has wings that jut out on both sides, making it seem even longer. There are gables and steeples all over the main building that reach up into the sky, giving it a Gothic flair.

Standing at the edge of the campus, I look out onto the grounds, noticing the smaller, more modern-looking buildings scattered about—and how one of them is only a short distance away.

Liza is practically shaking—from the cold or from nervousness, I have no idea. "How are you doing?" I ask her. "Do you want to borrow my scarf?"

I'm just about to take it off when I notice a spotlight blink over what appears to be a garden of overgrown deadness—dry and twisted trees, and walkways spilling over with bushes from hell. "Did anyone see that?" I ask, completely focused on the spotlight, on how it seems to be fully illuminated now.

"See what?" Tony asks.

I shake my head, deciding to just keep it to myself.

Even though the main building is still a good three hundred yards away, it seems so close. And I suppose it is. I mean, it's one thing to see this place from the back of a mini-golf course, when it's far enough away to crack jokes about shock treatments and straitjackets and not feel self-conscious doing it. But it's a completely different thing when it's sprawled out in front of you like a castle. When you probably shouldn't even be here, let alone say anything disrespectful.

Still, there's just something about this place that calls out to me, like it wants to invite me in. And I'm nuts enough to actually go.

I glance around some more, trying to see if I can spot any security guards anywhere, but the buildings and campus look pretty deserted, so I'm thinking they must be hanging out around the entrance off Route 62, on the opposite side of the building, Dunkin' coffee and crullers in hand, fighting to stay awake. I mean, how can a place so immensely huge be completely guarded by cops? Still, the idea of sprinting our sorry selves across an open lawn doesn't give me a warm and fuzzy feeling, either. I mean, we're bound to get bagged.

"We shouldn't be here," Liza whispers, before I can thwack a little sense into our tour guides.

"There's no turning back now," Mimi says, lifting her ski mask to just above eye level. She takes out her pocketknife, and for a second I think we're all done for, but then she orders us to stay put—all of us except Derik, who follows her with the camera to the building closest to us.

"This better be worth it," Greta says, straightening out her skirt. She's got the thing hiked up around her waist for trekking purposes, a pair of dark tights underneath.

"Just remember," Tony says, "a lot of self-respecting A-listers started out in horror films. Just look at Paris Hilton."

"You are not seriously comparing me to *her*, are you?"

Before Tony can answer, Mimi gives us the thumbs-up. "We're in," her voice plays through the walkie-talkie.

"Come on in," Derik's tells us. "But be quick and be quiet."

We go—some a bit more reluctantly than others. While Tony tries to soothe Greta, continuing his list of respectable actors in horror films, Liza is still shivering. I unravel the scarf from around my neck and go to hand it to her, but the wind blows it from my grip. It ends up tangling into a mass of brush.

"What's going on?" Derik calls from the door.

"We shouldn't be here," Liza repeats.

"Don't worry about it," I tell her. "You can stick with me. You can be the ice cream and I'll be the nuts on top. We can be like Nutty Buddies."

"No," she says. "You don't understand. I already feel it. This place isn't right."

I suck in my lips and nod, doing my best not to flip out. Because there's a big part of me that knows she's right. But an even bigger part that wants to go in and see what this asylum is really all about.

DERIK

WE ENTER THROUGH a side door of one of the outer buildings. Mimi is able to pick the lock pretty easily, putting me to shame. The girl has some seriously hidden talents. Once inside, we take a few steps down into what appears to be a basement, and click on our headlights.

"Anybody trip over a grave marker on their way up here?" Mimi asks.

I shoot her an eye-dagger, hoping it'll shut her up—I mean, we've barely even made it inside yet. But Mimi's got this wide-ass grin across her face like the idea of freaking people out gets her off.

"What grave markers?" Liza asks. "I didn't see any graves."

"They didn't always use them," Mimi explains.

"It's all about downsizing," Chet says, trying to make light of it.

Mimi smiles wider, stoked for the attention. She gets

right up into Liza's face: "People who were patients and died here, people whose families didn't claim them because they were too ashamed to have a relative in a mental institution, were buried nameless; just a number in the dirt—and now it's all overgrown. I bet you didn't even notice."

"That can't be true," Tony says.

"It *can be*, and it *is*," Mimi corrects.

"No wonder this place feels so haunted," Liza whispers, looking around.

"Don't listen to Mimi," I say, grateful for the drama but knowing that Mimi needs to keep her trap shut before I have everyone backing out on me. I keep a good grip on the camera and move deeper inside the basement, glad when the others do the same.

The place is a shitty mess. The windows are all boarded up. And there are cans stockpiled everywhere, file folders and papers dumped out all over the floor, and old medical equipment—microscopes, stretchers, bed trays—strewn about the place. Mimi picks up a folder and starts paging through the contents.

"Anything eBay-worthy?" Chet asks her.

Mimi ignores him and closes the folder back up. She tucks it inside her coat for a later look and continues to pick through a bunch more.

"Could it be any colder?" Greta asks, rambling on about how freezing her legs are.

"Maybe next time you break into an asylum in the

middle of winter, you should go for pants," I offer, noticing the door at the back of the room.

"Next time?" Her eyebrow arches up. "I think not."

"We thought a lot about our wardrobe." Tony gives the hem of his black leather jacket a good tug. "Our goal was sexy yet sophisticated, sleek but not too flashy."

Yeah, thanks for telling me, I want to say. But instead I hold it in, taking a second look at Tony's crazy-tight black turtleneck—to show off his ten-year-old-boy chest and matching arms. The guy can't be more than ninety pounds soaking wet, and at least twelve of those pounds are for his hair—a huge dark mass of curls just begging to get hacked off. If he had a mustache, I'd be calling him a seventies porn star.

Meanwhile, Chet tries to make fun of the near-Siberian weather, smoking an invisible cigarette; the cold air puffs out of his mouth and floats across his flashlight beam, looking like actual smoke.

"Do you think it's extra cold because of ghosts?" Greta asks, aiming her headlight at the wall. Someone's spray painted the words *Screw you, Security* across the paint-chipped bricks. "I saw this documentary once where a ghost hunter guy said that paranormal activity makes places really cold."

"Well, duh," Mimi says, still picking through the files. "I mean, we *are* in a basement. Ghosts are notorious for haunting damp and dark places."

"Speaking of damp," Tony says, "what's with the

puddles on the floor?" He checks the heels of his Aldo boots and makes a face.

"Hundred-year-old piss," Chet says. "Nothing else I know stenches this bad."

"You obviously haven't smelled your own breath," Greta shoots back.

"Let's go," I say, cutting through their shit and trying to lead them toward the door at the back. I pull the map out of my pocket and go to angle my headlight over it, but the damn bulb keeps flickering. I smack it a couple times, and finally it stays on.

A second later, we hear a knock at the basement door—the same door we're headed for, the one that leads into the tunnel.

"What the hell was that?" Greta blurts.

I place my finger over my lips to quiet everybody and then I move closer to the door and press my ear up against it. I can hear a faint pounding sound coming from somewhere in the tunnel. "I'll bet it's just a heat duct," I tell them, thinking how the one in my house makes a hell of a racket.

"That was *no* heat duct," Tony says, all defensive. "Someone was knocking."

"Plus," Mimi chimes in, "the heat isn't even on. The place is vacant, *remember?*"

"Right," I say. "No one's here."

"Just ghosts," Liza whispers.

"Lots and *lots* of ghosts," Mimi says, arching her

eyebrows. She stuffs a couple more files into her coat, making me wonder what she plans to do with them.

"There's nothing here," I insist, for Liza's sake. "Look, I'll show you." I pull the door open, the hinges creaking like a crypt, and cast my headlight down the tunnel. It's dark and narrow with a series of arches that span the entire way. The walls are made of bricks, all painted over with white, but now chipping in places and covered with graffiti. An overhead pipe leaks water onto the floor, making a dripping sound. "See?" I say, trying to get a grip. "It's vacant."

"Holy yuck," Greta says, peering down the tunnel.

I aim the camera at Liza's face. "Are you okay?"

She shakes her head. "I really think we should leave. This place doesn't feel right. It doesn't want us here."

"How do *you* know?" Mimi asks, giving her lip ring a tug.

"Trust me," she insists. "I want to go back."

"Not funny," I say, feeling a chill pass over my shoulder.

"I'm not joking. Can you take me home?"

"Now?"

"We can't go back now," Mimi says. "We're here. We got in."

"It doesn't feel right," Liza snaps, enunciating the words like nobody's really hearing them.

"We could drop her off home and come back," Chet says. "Or, *I* could just drop her off. . . ." He snakes his arm around Liza.

"Yeah, right," I say, totally getting his play. The guy thinks he's a freakin' superhero.

"If we leave, I refuse to come back," Greta says, repositioning her beret so that it sits crooked on her head. "I'm sorry I even agreed to this thing in the first place. I didn't even have time to squeeze in an appointment for highlights. My hair's going to look totally over-the-counter Clairol in this lighting."

"I'm starting to regret it myself," Tony says, holding his flashlight high, way above his head, as though trying to light up the shot.

I lower the camera a second, trying to decide what to do. It'd totally suck to botch this thing. I mean, this is my future we're talking about here.

"Get a grip," Mimi says, approaching Liza from the mound of files. "Think how much stronger you'll be as a result of this."

"You don't understand," Liza argues. "This isn't my kind of thing. My parents think I'm at a sleepover, for God's sake."

"Oh, and what, this is *my* type of thing?" Mimi says. "Or any of us, for that matter? You're not the only one who's scared, you know."

"You can stay close to me," Chet whispers to Liza.

"She'd be safer on a shock treatment table," Mimi says, pulling Liza away from Chet, like Liza's a wishbone or something.

I angle the camera to zoom in on Liza's face, adjusting

the shotgun mic so that it's positioned outward to pick everything up.

Liza looks right at me—right at the camera. "Please?"

I let out a sigh and lower the camera back down. "Are you serious?"

She nods.

"If *she* goes, *I* go," Greta says, pulling a cobweb off her shoulder. "I mean, I know about low budget, but this is downright hokey. What kind of director has his cast walk out on him barely an hour into the shoot?"

"Look," Tony says. "I think what Greta is trying to say is that, while we're all for supporting independent film-making—"

"Please," I bark, cutting him off. I focus hard on Liza. "This place is gonna be torn apart in a few days. I don't have time to get another crew. I need you guys." I place the camera on the ground, fighting the urge to hurl it against the wall.

"Well, I'm not going anywhere," Mimi says.

"And how about the rest of you?" I ask.

But none of them even looks at me.

"This is my only chance," I say, running my fingers through my hair in frustration. "Don't you get it? If I screw this up, I'm stuck working in a diner for the rest of my life."

"What are you talking about?" Tony asks.

"Forget it," I say, grabbing my camera. I go to pack it up and get the hell out, but Liza approaches me.

She nudges my hand away from the off switch, making my heart beat fast. "Leave it on," she says finally. "I'll stay."

"Are you sure?" My lips shake just forming the words.

Liza stares at me, her giant green eyes filled with fear. I feel like a complete and total asshole for even *thinking* about letting her stay. "I'm sure," she says, not sounding like she's sure at all.

But she moves into the tunnel anyway.

DERIK

WE BOOT IT THROUGH the door at the back of the basement and enter into the narrow tunnel, the smell of rot and decay plugging up my nose, making me want to yack. Paint is peeling everywhere, and chunks of the ceiling have fallen onto the ground. I maneuver through it all, following the paint-splotched signs for Building A, noting how the writing is red.

Like blood.

Like some bad horror flick.

The perfect setting for my movie.

The banging sound continues, but I can't tell where it's coming from. My headlight continues to flicker. I stop and smack the thing again.

"Did you bring extra batteries?" Tony asks.

I shake my head, pissed at my own stupidity, but luckily the light starts working.

"Listen for a second," Greta says. "Did you hear that?"

"What?" I turn toward her.

"I thought I heard something squeak." She points to a door, like for a utility room or something. It's open a crack.

"I don't hear anything," Tony says.

"Maybe it was a rat," Chet says. "You gotta assume a place like this has got some dog-sized ones."

"Or human-sized." Mimi shoots Chet an evil smile.

We listen for a couple more seconds, but it's just dead silent. Then we hear music—the sound of a little girl's voice singing Happy Birthday, making me almost shit myself.

"Sorry," Greta says, grabbing her cell phone and checking the caller ID. "It's just my ringtone."

"Nothing like a little evil children's music to lift the spirits," Chet says.

"Who is it?" Tony asks.

Greta smiles, checking the number. "Don't worry about it," she says, stuffing the phone back into her bag.

But Tony doesn't let up, continuing to try and get her to spill it about the phone call. Meanwhile, I lead everyone forward through the tunnel, surprised that a cell phone would even get reception down here.

My shoes are drenched from stepping through puddles, making it feel even colder, despite how fast we're moving. Finally, we get to the end of the tunnel, to the main building. I lead them up a staircase. It's falling apart in places; some of the steps have collapsed. There's a rusted metal fence that divides the staircase in two—to separate the men and women, maybe, or maybe the crazies from the even craziers.

"Where are we going?" Tony asks.

I stop a second at the top of the stairs, angling my headlight over the map, trying to figure things out. The place is a freakin' maze. "We need to find the reception room," I say, noting how far away it is, how it seems you need to access it from another floor. "I thought we could start there—use it as a meeting place."

"I want to look around first," Mimi says, peering down the long corridor. There are rooms to the right and left. A clock hangs off the wall, the time stuck in place at quarter till three.

I nod, eager for the footage, noticing how Liza seems a bit more together now. "Are you sure you're okay with this?" I ask her.

But instead of answering, she steps away—into one of the patient rooms. Greta and Tony, still arguing, do the same, moving into the room directly across the hallway from her. And Mimi moves into a room a couple doors down.

"If anyone needs a little something to ward off evil spirits, now's the time to ask." Chet pulls a necklace of garlic from his duffel bag. The thing is huge; I'm surprised he even got it in there. He hangs it around his neck and poses for the camera. I'm tempted to call him on it—to call him the buffoon that he clearly is—but when it comes right down to it, I'm glad he's here, that someone like him is around to lighten up the mood a bit.

"I'm all set, man," I say, hearing the banging sound again. My heart pumping hard, I step into one of the rooms, noting how tiny it is. I wonder how someone could stand to stay in here for five short minutes, never mind spend a couple or twenty years.

The walls are peeling—huge curls of paint flaking off everywhere. You can see a ton of paint bits and chunks on the floor, as well as debris from the ceiling. There are a bunch of beds crammed in here. I take a step toward the one in the far corner, noticing a series of scratches on the wall right beside the headboard. Zooming in even sharper, it looks like maybe the scratches are from the bed. I can almost picture it, can almost see some nutjob lying here, all strapped down, trying to get out—writhing like crazy . . . but no match for the harness.

I move in a little farther, drawn to it—to the scratches— like I have to touch them, like I have to feel where the paint was scraped off. I reach out and move my fingers slowly toward the wall. A second later, I feel a hand tap my shoulder, totally making me jump.

I turn around. It's Mimi.

"What the hell are you doing?" I shout.

"Sorry," she says, a huge-ass smile across her face—like she isn't sorry at all. "I was just checking up on you."

I shake my head, trying to get a grip. My heart thrashes around inside my chest.

"Big strong man like you," Mimi says with a grin. "I didn't think your kind *could* get scared."

"Not scared," I correct. "Just surprised."

Yeah, right.

"What were you doing?" Mimi asks.

I look back at the bed, at those scratches, still tempted to run my fingers over them. But instead I shake my head. "Just checking things out," I say, taking a deep breath. I notice a book on a bedside table, the bookmark stuck somewhere in the middle, like whoever it belonged to never got the chance to finish it.

"Sad, isn't it?" Mimi says, motioning to the barred windows, now boarded up with pieces of plywood. "The bars were so they couldn't jump out, I guess. I mean, what else *would* you want to do if you had to stay here?"

"I guess," I say, zooming in on the graffiti. A bunch of people have marked the territory with their names. Somebody's even drawn a picture of a tombstone with the number seventeen on it.

Mimi sits down on the edge of one of the beds and runs her hand over the mattress. "It's almost like you can feel them," she says. "All the people who slept here."

"I'll take your word for it," I say, holding back from calling her the nutcase that she clearly is.

Mimi gets up and continues to poke around, checking underneath all the mattresses. I follow her with the camera to see what she finds—an old pack of cigarettes, a box of old crayons, some candy wrappers, an ancient copy of *Good Housekeeping* magazine. She moves to the bed in the corner, the one that made those scratches.

"This is just like that Brad Anderson movie," she says. "Did you see it?"

"*Session 9?*"

She nods. "Pretty freaky, huh?"

"Definitely," I say, remembering the film—about a clean-up crew hired to remove asbestos from this very hospital. I rented it one night with a couple of my buddies. The crew ended up going crazy by the end of the movie. And a bunch of people got killed. "But that would never happen in real life," I say, and wait for her response.

But for once she doesn't have one.

"Hey, check this out," she says, working a slit at the bottom of the mattress, right beside the seam. She goes to stick her hand inside.

"Are you sure you want to do that?"

She nods, continuing to maneuver around in there, pulling out a hair comb and some change. But then her face lights up when she feels something big. She pulls it out.

A notebook, all wrapped up in wax paper.

"Jackpot," she says, smiling like it's her freakin' birthday. She tears off the wax paper covering, opens the notebook up, and starts to read:

March 5, 1981

This is my second day at the castle, that's what everybody calls this place. I guess it sort of looks like one, except the rooms are tiny. There's not even enough room between my bed and the person's next to mine to manage a leg. So you can't walk between. You have to crawl across the foot of the beds when you want to go to sleep.

They took my shoes. And they dumped out my suitcase and took all my clothes. Some red-haired woman told me I'd get them back, but I didn't understand when. Then some doctor asked me all these strange questions: What year it is, if I know my name, if I could tell the color of his shirt.

But then he asked me if I wanted to die.

I told him that sometimes I do.

And then he sent me to the A wing without so much as another word.

More later.

"Pretty cool, huh?" Mimi says, closing the notebook.

"If that's what you want to call it."

"Oh, come on." She rolls her eyes. "You can't tell me that didn't give you tingles."

"Not exactly my idea of tingle-worthy," I say, watching as she shoves the notebook into her coat for a later look. "Just help yourself."

"What do you care?"

I shrug, pretending like I could give a shit. But the truth is, for some reason it does kind of bother me.

A moment later, Liza walks in.

"Hey," I say.

"Hey." Her bottle-green eyes look right at me, like maybe she doesn't completely despise me.

I focus the camera so that it zooms in on a wall full of old and yellow-stained photographs, all corroded and rotted: a picture of an older couple holding a giant codfish, a photo of someone's dog taking a piss, a picture of someone's totaled Corvette, a Polaroid of a little girl with missing teeth. There's also a bunch of magazine cutouts: an apple with a bite missing, and people posing in seventies clothing, like right out of a Sears catalogue.

"So weird," Mimi says.

I nod, wondering what the pictures mean—if any of these people are the person whose thrashing around on the bed made all those scratches on the wall.

A moment later, the door slams shut, freaking me out. It's Chet.

"Anybody for a little brain play?" He's got that stupid brain cap on again, and he's holding something long and pointy high above his head.

"What the hell is that?" I ask, angling my camera at it.

"Is it a knitting needle?" Mimi asks, grabbing it out of Chet's hand.

"Beats me. What do I look like, Martha Stewart?"

"Now that you mention it," I say.

"What can I tell you?" Chet says, ignoring my remark. "I found it in one of the rooms."

"Doubtful," Mimi snaps. "They wouldn't let patients get their hands on something sharp like this."

"Fine, don't believe me," Chet says, grabbing the needle back and stuffing it into his duffel bag. "But this baby's gonna bring me some fine booty on eBay."

"The only booty *you'll* ever get," she zings.

"You're seriously gonna sell it?" I ask.

"Are you kidding? I plan to sell whatever I can cram into my bag."

Before I can even respond, Mimi steps toward Chet. He opens his arms, thinking she's gonna give him some action or something, but instead she moves behind him, staring at something on the wall by the door.

"What is it?" Liza asks.

I look, too. There's a watercolor picture tacked up, the edges all curled and yellow with age. It's of a girl with dark stripes of hair and gigantic purple eyes. The twisted part is that the girl is missing chunks of herself—like, she only has one arm, half a set of hips, and she's missing her mouth entirely. She doesn't have any feet, and someone's torn her heart right out—you can see the tear marks in her chest.

"It looks kind of like me," Mimi says.

"Last I noticed, you had *all* your parts." Chet growls, giving her ass a wink like it can talk back.

"No," Mimi barks. "I mean, it looks like the way I used to paint myself—the hair, the eyes. I always forgot to draw in the feet, too." She rubs the picture with the palm of her hand, trying to smooth down the curled-up edges. Then she peels the thing off the wall, turns it over, and reads the back: "C. B. February, 1982."

Mimi caresses the thing the way a twelve-year-old boy does with his dad's stash of dirty magazines.

"Are you okay?" I ask her.

"Yeah," Chet says. "Maybe the asbestos is getting to you."

But before Mimi can get into it with him, I suddenly realize: "Where's Greta and Tony?"

The others stare back at me with blank expressions, like they don't know either.

I fling the door open and boot it down the hallway, shouting their names a bunch of times.

But no one answers. All you can hear is the echo of my voice. And that endless banging racket.

I hurry as fast as I can, more pissed by the minute. I check a bunch of rooms. No luck. I move farther down the hallway, my headlight beginning to falter again. "Where the hell are they?" I shout, nearly dropping the camera.

All of a sudden, out of nowhere, I hear someone scream behind me.

It's Liza.

I look back. She's got her hands gripped over her mouth. "I just saw a rat!" she screeches.

"Come on," I say, and turn back, continuing to look for Greta and Tony.

One of the rooms toward the end of the hallway has its door closed, totally tipping me off. I go for the knob, but it just jiggles back and forth, refusing to open. "Tony!" I shout, pounding my fist against the door. I try the knob again. This time it turns, and I throw the door open.

But the room is empty. All except for a rubber doll. It hangs by a noose from the center of the ceiling, making me almost piss myself. It's swinging back and forth slightly, like someone just pushed the thing. Even though there's nobody here.

I take a deep breath, wondering if the rush of the door made the doll move like that; if there's an open window. I peer toward the back of the room, but everything's boarded up.

"Baby Debbie likes to cry," a voice says, making me jump. It takes me a second to realize the voice is coming from the doll—from the *fuckin'* doll!—one of those talking ones. It's got a high-pitched voice with a grainy sort of quality, like an old, static-filled tape.

I aim the mic right in the doll's direction, my fingers shaking, wondering what kind of twisted shithead would take the time to rig up something like this.

The doll's just staring at me—right into my camera— all dirty, with crazy messed-up blond hair and tilty blue eyes, the kind that open and close.

"Baby Debbie wants to die," the voice continues. At least I think that's what it says. It's even grainier the second time; the words are all drawn out like her battery's dying.

A few seconds later the doll starts laughing.

"Holy shit!" I shout, backing away.

I go to touch the thing, to look for a tape recorder, but

the laughing gets louder, like the thing has a mind of its own. "What the fuck?" I shout, my heart beating fast.

"What's wrong?" Mimi calls, from somewhere down the hall.

I don't answer. I just shut the door and move away, down the corridor, trying to pull myself together, to forget I even saw it, even though I can still hear that twisted little laugh.

I stop at the very last room at the end of the hallway, my adrenaline pumping something fierce. That's when I find Tony and Greta. They're standing at the foot of a mattress. Greta's got her hands around Tony's neck as though she's just about to plant him one.

"What the hell do you think you're doing?" I shout, aiming my camera right at them.

"*What?*" Greta asks, annoyed by the interruption.

"We just wanted a little privacy," Tony explains.

"Are you guys deaf?" Mimi asks, butting her head in. "We've been calling you!"

"You can't do that," I bark, not giving them time to answer. "You can't just take off like that."

"Why?" Tony asks, his voice all high and whiney. "What's the big deal? We were only at the end of the hall."

"The big deal is that this placed is messed up," I say.

"What happened back there?" Mimi asks me again.

I tell them about the doll I found, adding that the rush of the door probably made the thing waver back and forth, that there must have been some sensor thing hidden under the doll's dress—something to detect motion, causing the tape recorder to trigger at just the right time.

"Did you actually see a recorder?" Tony asks.

I shake my head.

"Let's go check it out," Mimi says.

I shake my head, telling myself that there *had* to be a recorder. That's the only logical explanation. "I want to keep moving forward."

"Hey, is this where the party's at?" Chet asks, behind me now. Liza stands beside him, her face all white like she's just seen a ghost.

"Obviously some of us decided to have our own private party," I say, gesturing to Greta and Tony, still standing only inches apart.

"Cut them a little slack," Chet says. "I can see the appeal—barred windows, piss-stained mattress." He gestures toward the rubber mattress on the floor.

"Visual stimuli," Mimi adds, nodding at the giant penis spray painted on the wall. She goes over to the bed and checks out all four sides, hell-bent on finding more crap.

"Shouldn't you be wearing gloves?" Greta asks her.

"Probably," she says, trying to pull one of the mattress seams, without any luck. She lets out a sigh and looks toward the door. "Hey, this is one of the seclusion rooms." She points to the tiny square window at the top of the door where people can peep in. "They stripped people down and threw them in here as punishment."

"Sounds kind of hot," Chet says. "Anybody for a reenactment?"

"Let's go," I say, still thinking about that messed-up doll. "We need to stay together."

Or else something heinous is gonna happen. I just know it.

MIMI

THIS PLACE IS DARKER than I ever imagined. Not dark as in black—though it's plenty black, too—but dark as in morbid. Sad. Eerie beyond belief.

It's not just about the mess, either. It's about everything. It's about the pieces of those who stayed here—the pieces left behind.

Like the rotted deck of cards.

And the dress with the burned sleeves.

The torn bedsheets.

And the shredded lace curtains hanging over the barred-up windows.

The corroded walls with peeling paint.

And the signs on every door we pass through:

BEWARE, PATIENTS WILL ESCAPE!
EXERCISE EXTREME PRECAUTION UPON ENTERING!
WARNING: MAKE SURE THE DOOR IS SHUT
AND LOCKED BEHIND YOU!

With each one, I get this weird little knot in my gut. Like, even though the place is vacant, I feel as though something's behind these doors—some pent-up, angry energy just busting to get out.

Derik leads us up and down several flights of stairs, exploring the various wings until some of them begin to blur together. This place is like one giant mouse maze.

We end up in some back area, where all the really disturbed patients lived. I know because there's nothing more than a bare mattress on the floor—and all the windows have bars.

No curtains.

No pillows.

No bathrooms.

You can still smell the stench of human waste.

I pick up a bunch of patient file folders along the way, as well as some other relics I come across: a journal, a clown mask, an old magazine, a bar of soap with teeth marks embedded into the side.

And a watercolor picture—one I just had to have.

We follow Derik into a room, where a bunch of kids obviously had some fun. The walls are all painted over with bloodred splotches. And someone's written the words: "Christine Belle died here. Her body is buried out in the garden."

"Christine Belle," I whisper, looking down at the watercolor clutched in my hand. I flip it over to view the initials C. B., knowing somehow that it's the same person. The eeriness of it—of the coincidence, maybe—sends a chill right through the center of my skull. If it's possible to even feel a chill there.

Liza turns away and waits by the door, like the possibility of the graffiti being true upsets her. Meanwhile, my focus shifts to the ground. The floor is littered with broken beer bottles, cigarette butts, and dirty old underwear.

"I need a break," I tell Derik, suddenly feeling weighted down by all my loot.

"*You?*" he asks, raising an eyebrow, like the idea of me needing a break surprises him.

"Ditto," Chet chimes in. "I need to take a leak."

"Break time!" Greta declares.

"Fine," Derik says, still working his camera. "Let's go."

Using the map, we move through several more wards and wings, up and down a couple more flights of stairs, through a couple rec rooms. We somehow make it to the reception room of the administration building, where we finally dump our bags.

"Okay," Tony says. "A short break, then how about we get serious? Film something really dramatic." He pulls what appear to be a stack of scripts and a director's megaphone from his bag.

"Are you kidding me?" I ask him. "This isn't *The Young and the Restless*."

"More like *The Young and the Sexless*," Derik says, motioning to Chet.

"Hey, what's that supposed to mean?" Chet asks,

standing so close to Liza that he might as well be humping her leg.

"It means stop molesting my cast." Derik takes a portable dolly out of his backpack and sets it up so that his camera rests on top.

"Wait." Greta throws her hand up as though to stop traffic. "Don't you want a high-concept, no-filler film? I mean, you don't want to bore people to death only ten minutes in, do you?"

Derik swivels the dolly to aim the camera at her.

"She's got that right," Tony says, using the megaphone, his voice echoing even more. "People will be asking for their money back before they even make a dent in their popcorn."

"Right," Greta says, striking a pose for the camera—hands on hips, back arched, stomach sucked in. "Which is why I was thinking we could have me act like I'm trapped in a room or something. I could be struggling to get out."

"Or maybe we could just have you trapped in a room," I suggest, faking a smile. "No acting required."

Greta lets out a huff, still overacting. "If I'm going to be involved in this project, I need it to have purpose . . . to have edge . . . to have *spice*."

"Spice?" Chet perks up.

Tony hands a script to each of us, but Derik totally ignores it, instead filming Greta's every bossy move.

"I thought we were supposed to be taking a break," I say, unzipping my coat to unload the tonnage of file folders I've squirreled inside, as well as the wax paper—covered notebook and the watercolor picture. I pile them on the floor, out of the way, and then pull a bunch of candles from my bag and set them up in a circle to establish a cozy area—if the word cozy could even apply here.

"Séance time?" Chet asks, rubbing his hands together.

"Yeah, I thought we could summon an evil spirit to take over your body and make you perform sadistic rituals."

"Sounds cool," he says.

I roll my eyes, noticing how Liza is sitting off by herself, eyeing my pile of stuff, probably wondering what my deal is. And so I listen to Chet ramble on about some candlelit picnic he attempted with a girl—how he accidentally burned his butt in the process—for exactly the length of time that it takes me to light all the candles. Then I join Liza, scooting in between her and my stack of file folders.

"Still feeling like this place doesn't want us here?" I ask.

"Make fun if you want."

"I'm not making fun. I'm just curious. What did you mean by all that?"

She shrugs instead of answering.

"You don't want to be here, do you?"

"Do *you*?" she asks. "Can you honestly say that this is fun for you?"

I shrug, wondering what she was thinking by coming

here in the first place—or if she was even thinking at all. "This place is definitely intense," I say, in an effort to play nice. "Part of it pulls you in. Another part wants to spit you out."

Liza's eyes lock on mine for just a second, and I almost catch sight of a trembling lip, like maybe she gets what I'm saying.

"Are you okay?" I ask.

But instead of answering, she looks at the watercolor I found.

"This place is screwing with you, isn't it?" I continue, pushing the picture toward her. "It's screwing with me, too. Just look at this painting. One minute I'm drawn to it; something tells me to pull it down, that I have to know more, and so I do, only to find the artist's initials on the back. Then, two minutes later, I see a name on the wall— a name that shares those *same* initials. I mean, it's quite a coincidence, don't you think?"

"I'm not sure I believe in coincidences."

"So you think it was intentional?" I ask, focusing on the place in the picture where there should be a heart. "Do you think that something greater—some external force, maybe—wanted me to make the connection?"

"External force?"

"Yeah. Like, maybe Christine Belle, maybe her spirit was reaching out to me. Maybe she's trying to haunt me." I flip the picture over to look at her initials again. Then I grab the journal from the stack of file folders. "I found this in the same room as the painting. It was wedged inside one of the mattresses. Do you want to read some of it with me?"

Liza stares at it, her mouth dropping open like she's seriously tempted. "Maybe not," she says finally, though unable to take her eyes off it. A moment later she gets up—just like that—as if the temptation is too strong and she has to get away.

Meanwhile, Derik's got the camera zoomed right at me. "We're heading downstairs to the tunnels," he says. "I want to shoot some of my storyboard stuff."

"Well, I want to take a break," I remind him.

"Break's over." He smiles. "Back to work."

"Not for me. I just sat down."

"Yeah for you," he insists. "Come on; we need to stick together."

"Why?" I balk. "I have a map. I have candles, a cell phone, a walkie-talkie, my flashlight—"

"*I* can stay with her," Chet offers.

"Oh. Yeah. I feel safe," I say.

"Liza, I'd like you to come, too," Derik says, practically drooling as she pulls the elastic from her ponytail. Her hair spills down in silky waves, totally making me want to hurl.

And I'm not alone. Greta rolls her eyes, pausing a moment from running a hairbrush through her curly dark locks. She uses the brush to thwack her beloved Tony on the side of his head. The boy has got his eyes seriously lodged right on Liza's chest.

"I was thinking we could get a cool shot of you holding a candle," Derik continues.

"I don't know," Liza says, chewing nervously at her bottom lip. "I may just want to sit for a little while to get my bearings—to get used to this place, you know?" She readjusts her hair into a grandmalike bun, but she still looks nauseatingly perfect.

"Maybe you *should* stay behind," Greta says, turning to Liza. "I mean, it's probably going to be super scary down there."

"Really?" Liza's eyes widen.

"Totally," Greta continues, feeding Liza's fear. "I mean, there's probably going to be all kinds of creepy stuff happening down there—blinking lights, faulty equipment, spirits passing through us. And we're probably going to be a while. We have a lot to shoot, so you might want to stay up here with the crew."

"That wouldn't mean more screen time for you," I ask, "would it?"

Greta shrugs, but my comment doesn't seem to bother her. "I guess now that you mention it, I could do that candle scene."

"Or *me*," Tony pipes up.

"Don't worry," Derik says, drawing his sweatshirt over Liza's shoulders *once again*—obviously a regular maneuver in his repertoire of playerisms. "Nothing weird is gonna happen down there. Liza can stay close to me."

Liza reluctantly joins him and the other two Hollywood wannabes. Tony is helping Greta get ready for her close-up at this very moment. He's got some powder out, dabbing it across her rounded cheeks and pointed chin. "So you won't shine for the camera," he says.

Meanwhile, I pretend to ignore them by thumbing through a bunch of file folders.

"Seriously, Mimi," Derik says, copping an attitude. "I'd rather you guys just came with us." He looks back and forth between Chet and me.

"Go!" I tell him, flipping open one of the folders. "I'll be fine."

"Let's go," Greta demands. She runs a fingerful of Vaseline over her teeth, muttering something about how it keeps her lips from rolling up into her gums when she smiles. Like lip-rolling is some regular occurrence.

"We'll be right downstairs," Derik says. "We're gonna go by way of the cafeteria. Use the walkie-talkie if you need anything."

"Sure," I say to appease him.

But Derik doesn't look so sure. Still, he leaves me alone.

Finally.

LIZA

IT'S ALMOST MIDNIGHT, barely two hours in this place, but I feel like I've been here for days. It's just kind of crazy . . . this sensation I have—like somebody's watching me. Ever since I set foot in this hospital, I've felt like there's someone standing over my shoulder, whispering into my ear, telling me that I shouldn't be here.

It's got me completely on edge.

It doesn't help that Mimi is making me nervous, too. I mean, I try not to judge people, but it stresses me out just looking at her—dark hair, dark makeup, shrouded in layers of black like it's Halloween. Like she truly enjoys excursions like this.

We'd barely even made it inside this place, and there she was, telling us all about some cemetery we passed—a noticeable twinkle in her eye. Then, only a few minutes ago, she asked me all these questions—if I believe in coincidence, if I believe in a greater power, and if I wanted to read some patient's journal she found.

She discovered the journal tucked inside a mattress in one of the rooms. I didn't tell her this, but when she wasn't looking, I opened it up and read one of the entries:

March 5, 1981

After dinner. There's a girl here named Jessica who really scares me. She's sixteen years old and she's got these dead black eyes and this really hard stare. She watched me while I slept last night. And so I couldn't sleep at all; I couldn't stop shaking inside. It felt like my skin was icing up. Somebody told me Jessica's in here because she hears voices. I can't even imagine what that must be like.

Still, my foster care counselor says this is a good place for me. The counselor at the emergency room said so, too. I don't know. The only thing I know for sure is that I want to go to sleep and never wake up. That's why I took those pills. But the treatments here are supposed to make me better. I just hope this place isn't as bad as my last foster home.

Or the one before that.

Or before that.

Or the girls home.

And maybe I can do my art again. Maybe I can even get my GED.

More tomorrow.

I don't know why I read that journal entry, or what compelled me to even open the notebook in the first place. There was just something that made me do it—a sudden urge that I can't quite explain.

But I guess I've been doing a lot of weird things since I got here.

Case in point, I stuck around when I could have left. I had the perfect opportunity to back out of this thing. Chet was even willing to drive me home. I mean, yes, I felt really bad for Derik. He's put so much energy into this project. And yes, I need this project myself—time's a-tickin' and I need to update my college applications with some extracurriculars.

But it was more than just pity and school. It was this place—the pull on me it had as soon as I stepped inside. Like, I want to go home but I need to see more. Like there's something bigger going on here than just abandoned buildings and debris.

Like exactly what Mimi said.

As if my internal struggle isn't unsettling enough, earlier, when Derik and the others weren't paying attention, I wandered into one of the rooms on my own and opened a closet. I found a noose in there. It was hanging down almost like an invitation. For just a split second something called out to me; I wanted to touch it.

And so I did.

With trembling fingers, I reached out and grabbed it, noticing my breath quicken and my legs start to shake.

I backed away right after I did it, wondering what I was doing, why I was still there.

Especially because the noose felt like death.

It was just like the watercolor picture that Mimi found. It called out to me, too. There was just something about it—the colors the girl used, the missing body pieces, the way the paper felt between my fingers. In that instant, sitting in the reception room when nobody was looking, I just had to touch it, to know more about the girl who painted it.

And so I can't help but wonder if maybe, like Mimi, I'm being haunted as well. The thought of it only makes me tremble more.

MIMI

ONCE DERIK AND the others leave for the tunnels, I start flipping through the folders, searching for my grandmother's name. Since she was once a patient here.

I know it's not rational. I know the odds of finding any trace of her are slim to none. I mean, there are files *everywhere* in this place. It's hard to walk and not step on somebody's medical history. But I have to try anyway. Because after my grandmother was admitted here, it's like her whole entire family forgot about her.

But I'm not forgetting.

I may not have been around when it happened (I hadn't even been born yet), but I'm here now. And this visit is long overdue.

My older sister Micki has only filled me in on bits and pieces of what happened. She says that our family became ashamed of it—the idea of having someone in an asylum. She expects me to understand, to see their side of things, to consider the fact that my grandmother was admitted here long ago—when people were more private about things.

But I *don't* understand. And actually, when I really stop to think about it, it makes me sick. Because, what if something like that ever happened to me? What if I needed to be institutionalized? Would my family forget about me, too?

And so my grandmother lived here.

And then died here.

And no one even bothered to visit her.

Until now.

Chet plunks himself down next to me. "Come here often?" he asks, giving me the smarmy eye.

"Is that supposed to be funny?"

"Come on." He laughs. "Where's your sense of humor?"

"I'm here, aren't I?"

"Yeah, but something tells me you're not in this for the laughs."

"Oh, really," I say, somewhat surprised by his perception. I mean, the guy's an absolute clown. To prove me right, he slips on the clown mask I found. It's the kind that has elastic across the back to hold it in place. A plastic version of Bozo, complete with a bulbous nose, happy lips, and fluffy red hair—even scarier than Tony's nest of thick brown curlicues and Chet's orange frizz put together.

The sight of it creeps me out. "Take that off," I snap.

"Not into clown kink, I take it." He takes the mask off.

"What's with the black eye?" I ask, ignoring his attempt at humor, remembering how Derik had asked about the black eye yesterday at the diner, but how Chet had laughed it off.

"First answer my question," he says. "What's with the chip?"

"Excuse me?"

He reaches over to rub my shoulder. "There's a pretty bad one right there."

It takes me a moment to get it, and when I do, I can't help but smile. "Pretty clever."

"A curse I have to live with." He smiles back, his light brown eyes crinkling up. It's the first time I notice the dimple in his cheek. "So what's the deal?" he continues.

"No deal."

"Something tells me you have an agenda," he pushes. "So what is it? Something more interesting than combat boots and a 666 attitude, I hope."

I shrug, glancing down at a profile sheet. "Gus Newman," I read aloud, avoiding the question. "Age seventeen. High school senior."

"Let me guess," Chet says. "Too much funny dust?"

"Social anxiety issues," I correct, reading from the chart. "It says here he had difficulty relating to his peers. Sound familiar?" I raise an eyebrow at Chet.

"Nope. Not to me," Chet says, using the clown mask as a hat now.

I flip through the pages, looking for something

meatier, some legitimate reason for Gus to be locked up in this place, but knowing that it happened all the time— that sometimes people got checked in for the wrong reasons. "I once read about this boy whose parents dumped him off here, saying he was too rambunctious for them to handle. A couple years here, and no word from his parents—and the boy really *did* go crazy."

"Sounds like something my parents would do."

"That explains a lot."

Instead of responding, Chet pulls the clown mask back down over his face and sticks his tongue out through the lips.

"Do you know how many germs that thing probably has?"

"Does that mean we can't make out later?"

"You *can't* be serious."

"Try me," he says, his tongue flailing away.

I go to rip the mask off, but Chet does it for me. "Maybe later?" he asks.

"There isn't enough mouthwash or money on the planet," I say.

At that he gets up, stretches his arms, and readjusts his headlight. "Playing hard to get? I like that." He winks.

"Wait, where are you going?"

"Just thought I'd pop over to the brain lab on my way to get some shock treatments."

"Seriously," I bite.

"Seriously, *come on*," he says. "Let's go for a walk. When

was the last time you were in an asylum? Let's be crazy!"

I flip another page in the folder. "I'm busy."

"Well, unbusy yourself. Because I have to take a leak, and you have to come with me."

"Not a chance," I say, making a face.

"Come on," he begs, dropping to his knees. "You need to protect me from the evils that lurk."

The boy makes me laugh. I want to despise him, but I'm too busy laughing at his lame-o jokes. After squabbling over it for a few more moments, Chet finally agrees to go wee-wee by himself. Still, he assures me that he'll be just down the hallway, by the cafeteria, and that if I need anything I should call him on the walkie-talkie.

Meanwhile, I continue to page through the folders, reading some pretty intense stuff: several people who thought they were Jesus, a woman who liked to eat toilet paper, a guy who thought he was a chicken, a bunch of people with multiple personality disorders, and a handful with schizophrenia.

I pause at this one lady's chart. It seems she had people inside her ranging in age from 1 to 101. I try to make out what the doctor scribbled on her treatment page, but then I hear something—a creaking sound behind me, like someone is moving across the floorboards.

I turn to look, but there's no one there—just a bunch of windows that are all boarded up.

"Chet?" I say, looking around. I pick up one of the

candles for added light. But I don't see anyone.

And so maybe I'm just hearing things.

I turn back to my reading, and reach for the journal. Even though it was kept in wax paper, it's still yellow with age. The corners are frayed and the back cover's almost completely torn off. Someone's decorated the front with decoupage—magazine cutouts of laughing children. Dozens of them. Little girls with open-mouth smiles and boys with huge, happy grins. But now there's an orangey-golden glaze that stains their faces, making them look almost sick.

I flip the journal open, noticing the name inscribed on the inside cover. It's written in pretty cursive, a vine of roses outlining the letters, and thorns digging in from all four sides—Christine Belle.

My skin tingles just seeing her name, knowing for sure now that the watercolor picture was indeed hers. I flip through a few pages, eager to read more about her.

But that's when I'm stopped.

"Mimi?" a voice whispers from somewhere out in the hallway.

My heart jumps. "Chet?"

But no one answers. And it's pitch black out there. My headlight only shines about eight feet, barely reaching the doorway.

"Chet, is that you?" I wait a couple seconds and then pick up my walkie-talkie. I press the TALK button. "Chet?"

But it doesn't seem to be working. I don't hear that

familiar static sound like before when we were in the woods.

My heart beating fast, I let out a breath, trying to get a grip, wondering if this is just my imagination. Or if maybe Chet is trying to get me back for not taking a walk with him.

I decide to ignore his lame attempt at scaring me, and focus on the journal:

June 10, 1981

It's a full moon tonight. And everyone here—all the patients—are wailing at the top of their lungs. It's the most chilling thing I've ever heard. You can probably hear the wailing for miles.

I look around as everyone does it. It's like a big game—who can sound the loudest. And yet the nurses don't even seem to care. Some of them think it's funny. Others ignore it, acting like they can't hear anything at all.

It makes me wonder if everybody's gone crazy.

I pull my blanket over my head, but it doesn't help. Jessica is right outside the covers, hovering over my bed, wailing as loud as she can to try and scare me.

And it's working.

My insides are shaking. My skin is cold. I want to be sick.

I take a deep breath, tempted to gouge my ear with this pen, to push it into the canal as far as it will go and draw a little blood. I bet it would win me a trip *to the doctor. At least then I could be with someone sane.*

Because this place is making me crazy.

More tomorrow.

I go to turn another page, but that's when I hear something else. The sound of water running.

"Chet?" I call out again, my voice sharper, more pissed off. I head out into the hallway, toward where the cafeteria is, my headlight shining the way. "You've got my attention now, asshole," I say, moving through the cafeteria doors, startled by the creaking sound of the hinges.

There's a giant oven right in front of me, and what appears to be a loading dock to the left. I move across the linoleum flooring, still trying to get my walkie-talkie to work.

But it's definitely dead.

"This isn't funny," I say, peering around the cafeteria. There are doors and windows along all four walls, making it look more like a hallway. The only real tip-off that this is a place where food was prepared are the giant mixing bowls—twelve of them—practically up to my waist. And the lingering smell of boiled cabbage.

"Come out *now*!" I call again. My voice echoes.

I move to the center of the cafeteria, noticing two separate dining areas—for the males and females, maybe. And then I notice the American flag. It looks like it's torn, like someone ripped the thing in two. But when I strain my

eyes, I see that it isn't an actual flag at all. It's just a picture of one. Someone's painted it on a door glass. But now
there's a hole it in—a big chunk missing—like someone
threw a rock.

I take a deep breath and continue to look around,
watching for a flashlight beaming or a shadow moving.
But it appears that I'm alone.

Even though I feel like I'm being followed.

I feel like there's someone standing somewhere behind
me, watching my every move. The skin at the nape of my
neck itches, like ants crawling down my back.

Breathing hard, I turn around—to head back to our
meeting place—but I smack into a table, whacking my
leg. Making a huge echoing bang.

I take another deep breath and try to calm the thump-
ing of my heart. Maybe I should head downstairs and see
if I can find Derik and them—tell Derik what an absolute
jackass Chet is being.

My leg throbbing, I move out into the hallway, back
toward the reception room, the smell of stale water—of
mildew mixed in mustiness—all around me.

"Mimi," a voice whispers again—a female voice. It's
followed by the sound of running water—even louder than
before.

"Who's there?" I call. "Liza? Greta?" Is it possible that
this is someone's stupid idea for a plot? That Derik has
agreed to let Greta and Tony take over with their stupid
scripts?

I clench my teeth, getting more pissed off by the moment. I mean, what the *hell*? This isn't what I signed up for—a bunch of high school adolescents playing haunted house in an abandoned asylum.

I peek into the reception room—still empty—and then head down toward the female wings, following the sound of the running water. It's getting louder with each step, leading me to a room at the end of the hallway.

"This isn't funny!" I shout, trying to remind myself that this is a joke, that there's some logical explanation.

"I'm not laughing," a voice breathes. I let out a gasp, but then realize the voice is coming from my walkie-talkie. I press the TALK button. "Chet?"

But the piece of crap goes dead again.

I reach into my pocket for my cell phone and try to dial. But it's not getting a signal.

My heart pumping hard, I move closer to the room. It's pitch black inside. "Chet?" I call out. "If you're in here, I'm going to kill you." I take a couple steps inside, wishing I had an extra flashlight or that I had brought along a candle. The narrow beam of my headlight shines over a bathtub. But it isn't running.

And there is no water.

But I can still hear the faucet; it sounds like the tub is filling up.

For hydrotherapy.

I step back, dropping my walkie-talkie. It makes a cracking sound against the tile floor.

Above the tub is a mural—a happy swan bathing in a pond with a fiery orange sun behind it—like that's supposed to make the hydrotherapy bearable. But even more twisted are the words splotched just above the scene, causing my skin to ice up, my heart to beat even faster. Written in dark red letters, the words "I've been waiting for you" puncture right into my heart.

And make me scream.

TONY

I LOVE MAKING GRETA jealous. She gets so mad. It's super hot on her.

Mostly because it makes her super hot for me.

Not initially. Initially she gets all pissy about it, but then she starts to come around—starts to realize that she can't always treat me like some second-rate actor. I'm an ace. And aces tend to have wandering eyes.

Before we came down here to the tunnel, I pretended to gawk at Liza. I mean, not that I *wasn't* gawking—*I was*—but I totally hammed it up. That's what we actor types do. We ham. I know it wasn't the nicest thing to do, but sometimes playing things up totally helps keep the spice in our already sizzling relationship. And honestly, who couldn't use a little added spice?

It's already paid off. Even though she's sulking, she's got her head resting on my shoulder as I shoot a scene between Derik and Liza.

```
INT. UNDERGROUND TUNNEL,
DANVERS STATE HOSPITAL - NIGHT

DERIK and LIZA, two attractive high
school seniors, stand at the end of the
tunnel, holding a candle between them.
ANGLE ON the shadow of the candle flame
as it lights up the walls, creating
tall, conelike shapes.
```

It isn't just my supposed lust for Liza that's got Greta all hot and bothered. She's also sulking because she wants to be the star of everything (including this scene), and, let's face it, there's really no reason she shouldn't be. The girl's got some killer talent, not to mention the most dazzling golden-brown eyes, the fullest pale pink lips, and the sexiest little tush I've ever seen.

```
PULL BACK to reveal GRETA, 17,
pouting those pale pink lips right
now.

              ME
Are you okay, babycakes?

Greta lets out a growl, still pouting.
```

Sometimes—*most* of the time—Greta hams it up, too. She has a hard time knowing where her character stops and reality begins. But I suppose all great talents have their flaws.

Plus, it's not like I didn't owe her a little suffering after how secretive she was about that phone call she got in the tunnel earlier. She still has yet to tell me who that was— though I can't say I was able to refuse her makeup nookie offering anyway.

I just hope she comes around soon—that she doesn't end up sulking for the rest of the night. The girl has a lot to be grateful for, after all. I mean, did I *not* score her a stellar monologue just as soon as we got down here? That's right; I talked Derik into filming her as she walked the length of the tunnel describing everything she saw. He didn't even object when she got totally into the role, acting like she was a patient trying to escape and chattering on about hearing voices and needing to feel the sun again.

```
CLOSER ON Derik and Liza, only inches
apart now, talking and smiling. Derik
leans in like he's about to go in for
some lip action.
```

I pull back slightly, making sure the volume is turned up all the way on the shotgun mic, wishing I could hear them better, but knowing that we'll get all the juice during playback time.

Derik and Liza really do make a pretty good-looking

couple—tall, lanky, athletic. Except, what is it with Derik's hair? Doesn't he know that nobody does that messy gel thing with their ends anymore? I run my palm over my well-groomed mane, grateful that it has body and texture all its own, wondering if Derik would be offended if I yelled out CUT and offered him a pointer or two.

DERIK

I'M STANDING WITH Liza at the end of the tunnel, our headlights off, just a candle between us. Since I've already gotten a good amount of footage down here, including a scene
of Greta doing a monologue (to get her and Tony off my
back), Tony's agreed to film this bit for me, saying that all
great directors make a cameo appearance in their movies.

Not that I'll even use this clip. I mean, it doesn't get
any cheesier than this: me and Liza are standing just inches
apart, facing one another, like at any moment I might slip
her some tongue or my breath mint of choice. I'm only
doing this scene to get close to her—I mean, *obviously*. But
who knows? Maybe if I stretch my imagination far
enough, I'll find my own personal use for the footage.

I stare right into her, watching the reflection of the
candle flame waver against her bottom lip. "Thanks for
staying," I say. "I mean, for a little while there, I really
thought you were gonna back out on me."

"Yeah, well, my guidance counselor told me I need to be a team player."

"Seriously? And that's what made you decide to stick around?"

Liza shrugs and looks away. "To be honest, I don't know why I'm here. I mean, normally I *would* have left."

"But you didn't; that's just it. It's really cool of you to hang around."

She shrugs again. "Maybe part of it was that thing you said before, when we first broke in—how this is really important to you . . . how screwing up isn't really an option. I know about pressure."

"You're really cool, you know that?"

"Don't be so sure." She shivers from a chill and pulls my sweatshirt tighter around her, a tiny smile curling up her cheek. "I'm apt to freak out at any moment. I mean, I don't know; this is all just a little too intense for me."

"Which part? The fact that we're standing in the tunnel of an asylum? Or the fact that you're doing it with me?"

She doesn't say anything at first, and so I'm thinking, Holy shit, this girl absolutely despises me, but then she finally answers: "The first one."

"Good answer," I say, venturing even closer to her, wondering if it's her that smells like vanilla, or the candle. "So what made you want to be a part of this, then?"

"Would you believe me if I said I thought it'd look good on my college application?"

"No way."

"Seriously," she says. "It's sort of a long story."

"Well, let's hear it."

"Maybe another time."

"Definitely," I say, wondering what she's all about, wanting to hear the rest of her story. And aching to kiss her.

But then Tony yells out "Cut!" Just when we were getting somewhere.

"Thanks a lot," I say, a bit of snap to my voice.

"No problem," Tony says, clueless to the snap.

He mumbles something about needing to fix my hair, but I ignore him, fastening my headlight back on and folding up the dolly. "We should really get back upstairs."

But before we can even start to backtrack, a scream rips through my walkie-talkie speaker. Making Liza scream out as well.

"That's Mimi!" Greta shouts.

I press the TALK button down. "Mimi, are you all right?"

But it doesn't seem like it's working now—there's just a weird buzzing sound coming from the other end. "Let's go!" I say, booting it down the tunnel. I reach for my cell phone and go to search for her number, but my cell is dead, too. "Shit!" I yell out.

We hurry down the tunnel, through all the rusted doors that line it, until we reach the steel door that leads upstairs. It's shut.

"Why's it closed?" Tony asks. "We didn't close it."

I try the knob, but it won't turn—like it's locked. "What the fuck?" I shout out.

Another scream rips through the walkie-talkie.

"Maybe the talkie's working now," Greta says, pressing the TALK button down. "Mimi? Are you there?"

Liza makes the sign of the cross.

Meanwhile, I set the camera down on the ground, angled toward us, and pound against the door with everything I've got. "Who the hell locked this thing?"

Tony tries to help me, but his ninety-pound frame only gets in my way.

I tell him to move and then take a couple steps back. I run and body-shove the door. But the thing won't budge. "We gotta go another way!" I shout.

"I think it's working now," Greta says, handing me her walkie-talkie. "I can hear voices on the other end."

I press it up against my ear. "It's Chet!" I can hear his voice. "Chet!" I shout into the thing.

But he obviously can't hear me, because I don't get a response.

"Piece of shit!" I yell, resisting the urge to chuck the thing against the wall. I try the door again. Still locked. "Let's go!" I say, grabbing the camera and moving in the opposite direction, hoping to find an alternate route upstairs.

"Let's check the map," Tony squeals.

I toss it at him and hurry down the tunnel. The walkie-talkie still pressed against my ear, I no longer hear any voices—just Liza's right behind me, whispering the Lord's Prayer.

I take a couple turns but end up at a dead end—the freakin' tunnel just ends—and we have to turn back.

"This place is a maze," Greta says.

"Wait, what's that noise?" Tony says.

We stop a second to listen. It sounds like a bunch of people talking—their voices whispering and whimpering together.

"Somebody's there," Tony says.

"It's pipes," I argue, noticing the water leaking through the cracks along the ceiling.

"That is *not* pipes," Greta shouts. "Someone's up there."

I strain to listen. It's like a constant whispering sound. "Just pipes," I insist, knowing that must be the truth.

"Let's go!" Liza insists.

"This way!" Tony shouts, using the map. He leads us to an open doorway. Beyond it is a stairwell that leads us upstairs. Someone's drawn a row of pissed-off angels, seventeen of them—their backs are numbered—climbing up the wall, heading for their doom. There's a picture of a devil at the very top. We sprint down a corridor and backtrack to the reception room.

"Where is she?" Greta shouts.

The reception room is empty now, all except for Mimi's circle of candles—still ignited on the floor.

DERIK

"GET AWAY FROM ME!" Mimi shouts. Her voice is coming from the D wing.

I tell Tony to stay with Greta and Liza and then I hurry down the hallway and around the corner—until I find Chet and Mimi.

They're standing in one of the rooms, facing one another. Nobody appears to be hurt, but Mimi looks pissed. "Get away from me!" she repeats, taking a step back from him.

"I'm sorry, okay?" Chet says. "It was stupid."

"What the hell happened here?" I ask.

But neither of them answers me.

"Hello?" I shout even louder. *"What happened?"*

"Chet's an asshole, that's what happened," Mimi says, finally looking up at me.

"What did you do?" I take a step toward him.

Chet turns to me. "It was just a joke. No big deal."

"What was a joke?"

"I was just taking a leak down here," he explains, gesturing to the tub. "I heard Mimi heading this way, so I hid behind the door and jumped out at her when she came in. No big deal."

"For your information," Mimi cuts in, "this is not a bathroom. They used it for hydrotherapy."

"Hydro-what-apy?" Chet asks.

"They made patients sit in the tub water for hours," she explains. "A canvas strapped over them so they couldn't get out. It was some warped idea of therapy."

"So what does that have to do with me?" Chet asks.

"Why don't you have a little respect?" Mimi says.

"I'm sorry, okay? I had to go, and the tub worked just fine—drain and all."

But Mimi is still flipping out, accusing him of trying to scare her way before she even headed down here. "I could hear you whispering my name," she says.

"What are you talking about? I didn't whisper anything."

"Don't play dumb," she snaps. "You were whispering my name. And I could hear the sound of water running."

"Maybe what you heard was the sound of me taking a leak."

"What's going on?" Greta asks, inserting herself into the action. She practically elbows her way past me so she can stand dead center, taking full advantage of the camera.

Liza and Tony are here, too—Liza practically glued to my side. Not that I mind.

"I'm not making this up," Mimi continues, rubbing her temples. "Someone was calling my name; someone even answered me. I said 'This isn't funny!' and someone answered, 'I'm not laughing.' It came through the walkie-talkie."

"Well, maybe that was one of us," I offer. "We could hear someone's voice coming through the speaker. Maybe you could hear us as well."

"Did one of you say that?" Mimi asks.

We all look at one another, but nobody seems to remember. I move even closer to Liza, sensing how freaked out she is. Her leg trembles against mine.

"I can't even remember what I said two seconds ago, never mind ten minutes," I say.

"Seriously," Chet says, turning to Mimi. "All joking aside; it wasn't me. I mean, aside from jumping out at you."

"Then who was it?" she asks.

"There's got to be some explanation," I say, giving Liza a reassuring squeeze, my arm wrapped around her shoulder. "It was probably just the talkie. You were probably either picking up on us, or maybe someone in the area. Those things probably have a killer radar."

"When they're actually working," Tony adds.

"Well, what about what happened to us?" Greta says, staring into the camera. "We were downstairs in the tunnel and the door closed and locked on us. We almost couldn't get back up here."

"This place is more than a hundred years old," I say. "What do you expect with heavy doors and rusted hinges?"

Chet goes to say something but then sees the writing above the tub. Someone's painted the words "I've been waiting for you" in bright red letters, making him pause. "This place is wacko."

"Exactly," Liza says. "Which is why we shouldn't be here."

LIZA

WHILE THE OTHERS sit around the circle of candles, taking a break, I sneak the journal again and read another entry, hoping that Mimi doesn't notice:

September 8, 1981

Last night I was punished. There's a woman here who murdered her husband. She got moved to my room, to the bed right next to mine.

And she scares me even more than Jessica.

I didn't want to sleep next to her, so I refused to go to bed. The next thing I know, four nurses came at me, ripped off my clothes, and threw me in one of the seclusion rooms in the back. I wouldn't stop kicking and screaming and punching the door, so they came back in, held me down, and injected me with something to make me sleep.

I hate this place. I hate the smell here—a mix of urine and bleach. And I hate most of the nurses. Some of them are so unbelievably cruel, especially to the older patients. They make them walk around naked—for ease, I think, so they don't have to keep changing them. And then they hose them down for cleaning.

A couple days ago, Vicky, this one crazy nurse, tied naked Mrs. Delaney to a chair with a bedsheet. Vicky kept her there pretty much all day, but Mrs. Delaney didn't complain too much since she'd been all drugged up.

Did I mention that I hate the drugs here? The pills I take make me jumpy all the time. Everybody tells me that I'll get used to the medication, that soon I'll settle in and make this place my home.

But I'll never call this place anything else but hell. The only good thing is that I've become friends with this one girl, Becky, who's in here because she kept plucking out all her hair. She wears a wig now, and her dad visits her at least a couple times a week. We go out on the terrace together sometimes for a smoke and talk about what we'll do once we get out of this place. She has all these ideas, but I can't think of one, so I just listen, and she doesn't seem to mind. She has a doll that she carries around all the time. It's made of cloth and yarn, so the nurses let her keep it. Plus, it's missing the button eyes, so there's nothing she can use to hurt herself. Yesterday, Becky asked me to draw eyes on the doll for her. I did, using black and blue fine-point markers, giving her the biggest, longest eyelashes a girl could ever have. Becky was so happy with the job I did, with the sparkly shade of blue I chose, that she renamed the doll after me—calling her Christy.

More tomorrow.

P.S. Tomorrow is my birthday. I'll be seventeen. Happy Birthday to me.

I close the journal and take a deep breath, wishing this were all one big dream that I could wake up out of, wondering how a girl my age could end up here. I glance toward Christine's watercolor again, focusing a moment on all the missing pieces—an arm, a hip, her mouth, the feet, her heart—and then I flip it over to look at the date. She painted it almost one full year after her first journal entry, making me wonder if this place only made her worse.

"What do you think?" Mimi asks.

My heart jumps just hearing her voice—realizing that she's been watching me all this time. The shadow of a candle flame flickers against her chin and crawls up her face, cutting it in two.

"Are you okay?" Derik asks, sensing my anxiety.

I nod, grateful for his concern. Contrary to what I'd heard about him prior to coming here, he's been really sweet to me, asking me how I am at every ten-minute interval. And sticking close by me.

"I think she haunts this place," Mimi says. "I think

she wanted someone to find her picture and journal."

"And I think you've been watching too many scary movies," Derik says, passing me an opened box of Cheez-Its.

I frown at it—at the idea of eating products that contain hydrogenated oils—but I take a handful anyway to be polite.

I go to pass the box to Tony, but he and Greta are way too busy arguing over some storyboards that he made up. Apparently Tony has his own ideas for how Derik's film should look.

"Who says this Christine chick is even dead?" Derik asks, distracting me from eavesdropping.

"That graffiti we saw on the wall," Mimi says. "Remember . . . the writing that said her body is buried out in the garden."

"But who even knows if that was true?" I ask for my own benefit. "Maybe it was someone who saw her journal and decided to be funny."

"Maybe. Maybe not." Mimi arches her eyebrows, like she can sense my discomfort—and enjoys it.

"Speaking of graffiti," Chet begins, "You know what I think is *really* weird?"

"The writing in the hydrotherapy room?" Mimi answers.

Chet nods, totally in sync with her. "Nothing like taking a whiz in front of a sign that says 'I've been waiting for you.' Talk about pressure."

"But it's true," Mimi says. "They *have* been waiting for us."

"Who?" I ask, somehow already knowing the answer.

"The spirits that linger here, the ones like Christine who can't move on."

"Do you think Christine's the one who wrote that graffiti?" Chet asks her.

"Are you kidding me, man?" Derik says, giving Chet's shoulder a push, "I can't believe you're getting sucked into this. I mean, I hate to be the one to break this to you, but last I heard, ghosts don't graffiti walls."

"How do *you* know?" Mimi asks. "Ever ask one?"

"Will you listen to yourself?" Derik aims his camera at her. "You're starting to sound a little weird, here—I mean, even weirder than usual."

"And that means *so* much coming from a stellar guy like you," Mimi says.

Derik peeks up at me, a bit embarrassed, maybe, because he quickly looks away. I can't help but wonder if the embarrassment is because of his reputation—if maybe he's afraid of my finding out about him.

Even though I already know.

"What do you think the spirits are waiting for?" Chet continues, obviously interested in all of Mimi's ghost talk.

Mimi takes a couple Cheez-Its and slides them into her mouth, over her stud-pierced lip. "I don't know," she says finally. "I mean, this place is going to be torn down next week. Maybe they need our help to tie up some unfinished business. Or maybe it's just a question of being heard of getting their stories told."

I look at Derik to catch his reaction, but he doesn't really have one. And so I have to ask him: "What do you think of that?"

"Of what?" he asks, looking back at me.

"Of being the one responsible for telling the story of this place?"

Derik's jaw tenses, as if the idea of it stresses him out. But he tries to make light of it: "You don't really believe all that stuff, do you?"

I shrug, honestly not knowing what to believe. I mean, logic would tell me that none of this paranormal stuff is true. But then why do I feel this compulsion to sink myself deeper into this place—to touch that noose, and feel that watercolor picture, and read from Christine Belle's journal?

And why do I feel like I'm being watched—like there are eyes in the walls, along the ceilings, and behind every doorway? I'm scared out of my mind, and yet I can't help but wonder what it would be like to wander down the hallway by myself, to go exploring in one of the wings, and to sit in one of the patient chairs. If the others weren't around, I'd probably be reading Christine Belle's journal right now—only stopping when I reached the very last word.

Derik looks back toward Greta and Tony, seeking a diversion maybe. It appears that she and Tony have made up. They've scooted away, into a corner of the room, sitting with their legs wrapped around each other. Greta whispers ething into Tony's ear, and he responds by kissing her lips, not once but *three* times.

"At least we've got ourselves a little entertainment," Chet says, stuffing the last of the Cheez-Its into his mouth and topping it off with a swig of Yoo-hoo. (Yoo-hoo = a nauseating blend of overprocessed milk, high fructose corn syrup, and cocoa.)

"More like a freak show," Mimi corrects, just a tad bit too loud.

"You're one to talk," Greta says between smooches.

Derik laughs, but Mimi looks hurt. She shrugs it off and focuses down at her black-polished fingernails—obviously not as tough and resilient as she'd like us all to believe.

"Did you know that there are close to three hundred germs in the human mouth?" I ask, trying to lighten things up.

"That's gross," Mimi says.

"But sharing your mouth with someone—kissing," I continue, "*does* help to support the immune system. Because, even though most of the germs in our mouths are the same, there's a small percentage of exclusive germs in there. Sharing those helps boost our immunity."

"Sounds like you've done your homework," Derik says.

"*I'd* like to do some homework." Chet raises his hand.

"Honestly, hornboy," Mimi says, "do you ever quit?"

"They don't call me Chet, the Energizer Honey, for nothing."

"Funny," she says. "I thought what they called you was Chet, the Energizer *Dummy*."

"You know you love me," Chet says, bumping her with his shoulder.

Oddly enough, Mimi doesn't object. She even has a quirky little smile curled across her lips. They end up moving away, into a faraway corner—peculiarly across from Greta and Tony—engrossed in conversation

"So," Derik says, sensing the sudden awkwardness. "Cracker Jack?" He holds the sailor-adorned box out to me as an offering. But even the promise of a prize inside doesn't tempt me.

"No thanks," I say, pulling a Balance Bar from my bag. "I think I've had my fill of food additives for the day."

"So you're a health freak?"

"Sort of." I shrug, tearing at the wrapper. "I'm going to be a doctor."

"For real?"

I shrug again, breaking off a piece of my bar for him. Derik pops it into his mouth. "It tastes like sandpaper," he says between chews.

"They call it Almond Brownie."

"Almond Sandpaper, maybe."

I smile and take a bite, noticing how, despite all this ghost talk, I'm feeling a bit more at ease—for the first time tonight.

"So how come you don't seem so excited?" he asks me.

"About what?"

"About working with drugs."

"Seriously?" I nearly choke on my Almond Brownie.

"No, I'm kidding." Derik smiles. "About getting to see people naked."

I can't help but laugh in response.

He grabs a bottle of water from his bag and passes it to me. "In all seriousness," he says, "how come you're not more excited about entering a profession with so many perks?"

"Because I'm scared that no colleges will accept me."

"Are you trying to be modest?" He positions the camera so that it points upward at us.

"I'm trying to be honest," I correct, following up with a sip of water. A trickle rolls down my chin.

"Well, I've heard about your grades," Derik continues. "I'm sure you'll get in *wherever* you applied."

"You'd be surprised."

Derik gives me a look—his eyebrows crinkling up like he just doesn't get it. I take another bite of my bar to avoid having to answer further probing, but now he's staring right at my mouth as I chew, waiting for some explanation. "Where are *you* going next year?" I ask, once I can swallow down.

"Red's Diner, ever hear of it? Best pancakes on the North Shore. And no food additives whatsoever."

"For real?" I ask.

He shakes his head. "Food additives are a cook's best friend."

"No." I smile. "I mean, are you serious about working at your parents' place? Didn't you say before that you *didn't* want to work there?"

He nods. "But unless something better comes up, I have no choice."

I glance at the camera, suspecting that *something better* has a lot to do with this project. Derik leans forward to click the camera off, and for one disappointing moment I think our conversation's ended.

But then I realize that things are just getting started.

"I want to be a filmmaker," he says, a shy little smile inching up his lip.

"Seriously? Like, for work?"

"Seriously," he says, staring at my mouth again. "For work."

"That's so exciting," I say, accidentally bumping my knee against his. He smells like citrus and candy—like something good enough to eat.

Derik goes on to tell me all about the contest he's entering, about how if he wins, his film will be shown on RTV. "It's just what I get really excited about," he says.

"That's great," I say, wondering what it feels like to be that excited about anything. Derik's pale blue eyes are wide, like I could jump right in. The feeling completely takes me aback—how close I feel to him, how excited I am just talking like this. It almost makes me forget where I am.

And who I'm with.

I think back to that time during our freshman year, when we were both standing outside the school, waiting for the bus. He was staring at me then, too. I could feel his eyes, watching as I turned the pages of my book. I knew he wanted to say hello, but he didn't. Of course, it didn't help that I ended up walking away, leaving him there because I was too nervous to say something interesting—or maybe I simply didn't feel I had anything interesting to say.

"Is it that way for you, too?" he asks, nudging in a little closer. The candle flame casts a shadow over his light brown hair. "I mean, what do *you* get excited about?"

I bite the corner of my lip, remembering how the guidance counselor had asked me almost the same thing. But the truth is, when you take away my goal of becoming a doctor, of going to Harvard, and studying my way to get there, there isn't much left—just a dull girl with an endless supply of health-nut trivia. A girl who doesn't have time for friends or boyfriends—whose last date was in the third grade, during a school field trip to the Museum of Science.

"It's not a trick question," Derik says. "I mean, do you get excited about medicine stuff . . . about playing doctor?" He smiles extra wide, making my cheeks heat up.

I give an enthusiastic nod, but it's nowhere near as enthusiastic as Derik's—the way he looked when he was talking about his film. "My parents and I have been planning this since forever," I say. "They bought me a real first-aid kit when I was eight years old. They let me tape up their fingers and wrap up their knees as practice."

"So *they're* excited."

I nod.

"And how about you?"

I open my mouth to say something—to give him one of my stock answers, something I've scripted for guidance counselors or admissions reps—but instead I just keep silent.

"It's okay if you don't know," Derik says. "I mean, my parents have got it all planned out for me, too. Sometimes it's easier not to think about it, to just go with the flow and let somebody else decide."

I nod, gazing at his mouth—at the pale pink color and the freckle on his upper lip—wondering if all those rumors about him are true.

"I'm glad you're here," he says, moving even closer to me. He takes my hands and presses his thumbs into my palms. And makes my heart beat fast.

He stares at me for several moments, and I notice how his eyelashes turn upward, how his eyes look so serious—like he needs to tell me something. And how his breath is warm against my chin. "I'm not sure what you've heard about me," he says finally, "but I think we have a lot in common."

"I'm glad I'm here, too," I say, knowing that we do have a lot in common and hoping to get to know him more.

DERIK

LIZA IS AMAZING. I mean, looks aside, the girl is sheer per-
fection: sweet, easy to talk to, likes to laugh. Not like one
of those girls who just nods her head and agrees with
everything I say, who says whatever she thinks I want to
hear. Or needs me to tell her what to think.

She's different.

It's like, when we're talking, she's really into it—she's
really into what I'm saying, like she's trying to figure stuff
out just as much as me. I mean, I never really saw myself
with some brainy girl, but Liza seems to get me in a way
that nobody else does.

I hold her hands, wondering if she notices how I can't
stop smiling—and how our lips are just inches apart. I'm
so into the moment that I don't even put up a stink when
Chet tells me that he's taking Mimi to the bathroom. I
don't even remind them that they need to stick together,
that they shouldn't veer off anywhere alone, and that they

need to bring their walkie-talkies. Instead, I focus on Liza.

"Are you cold?" she asks, staring right at me.

I shake my head, wishing we were alone, that I could be with her someplace nice. I pull a blanket around her shoulders, catching a waft of her vanilla scent. "I'd really like to get to know you better," I say.

"I'd like that too," she says, and she's smiling when she says it, like this could really be something good.

I watch her mouth, the way she keeps biting at her bottom lip, and wonder what she's thinking right now— if she's heard some of the stuff people say about me at school.

The truth is, I'm not like that anymore. Maybe I used to like the chase—to tag a girl and be done with her right after. But that's not me now. It hasn't been for the past six months, but it's like, once you have a rep like that, it's hard to shake it.

"So what do you say we hang out sometime?" I ask.

"Hey, don't we have a movie to make?" Greta barks, totally interrupting us. She untwists her legs from Tony's. The two have been squirreled up in the corner since we first sat down.

I pull away from Liza, a bit too quickly, maybe, wishing we had just a few more minutes alone.

"Hey, where did Mimi and Chet go?" Tony asks.

I feel my jaw lock, knowing that they should have been

back by now, that it's been a good twenty minutes since they left.

And that I never should have let them out of my sight in the first place.

CHET

IT'S MY IDEA TO SNEAK AWAY. While Derik is busy hitting on Liza—and Tony and Greta are busy hitting a homer—I suggest to Mimi that we grab our bags, tell Derik we're heading off to the bathroom, and then sneak away for a little urban exploration. What's surprising to me is that she doesn't object. But even more surprising is how cool the girl is. I mean, take away all the black clothes—and wouldn't I love to—Mimi is completely down-to-earth.

Oddly enough, the hardest part of sneaking off is resisting the urge to burst out laughing. But we manage, first moving slowly down the hallway, and then booting our asses well past the bathroom, toward the cafeteria. At one point, I reach out to feel for Mimi's hand, sensing her close by my side. Without even having to say anything—to tell her that my hand is extended out to her—she takes it, curling her fingers into my grip. And squeezing ever so slightly.

"Derik's going to have a fit," Mimi whispers, holding in her laugh.

"That's fine," I say. "Because I brought along my strait-jacket."

Still holding hands, we race across the cafeteria and open the door at the back of the kitchen. It leads to a back hallway, and straight ahead appears to be another tunnel.

"Let's go this way," I say, taking a left into a side room.

That's when things start to heat up.

Mimi closes the door so no one can hear us. Her back up against it, I'm standing there just facing her—one hand on the door panel, the other still cradled up in hers. And we're laughing like two little punks, like we just t-papered the principal's office or spread some computer virus through the school's administration records.

And then something really weird happens. Mimi looks at me for just a second—her violet eyes highlighted with these thick black rings. She tucks a strand of her kinky black hair behind her ear, and I notice how pretty she is— how her cheeks are sort of angular and her lips are the color of fire. I'm tempted to touch her—to glide my fingers down the side of her face and gently stroke her bottom lip. But then the corners of her mouth turn downward, like she knows how intense the moment is—like she wants the moment to end.

"So let's look around," she says, dropping my hand, just leaving me hanging.

"Yeah," I say, trying to mentally shower myself down.

The room is huge. There's a chalkboard at the front, and benches and tables overturned on the floor. I take a step, feeling something hard beneath my feet. I squat down to look. It's a dried-up tube of paint. And there are brushes, crayons, and bottles of glue littered about the floor. "It looks like this was an art room," I say, noticing the mildew-stained sketch pads piled high in the corner of the room. There are also works in progress set up on easels, and finished pieces displayed along walls.

"So what are we looking for?" I ask, thinking about all the booty these art supplies could get me on eBay.

"Files," Mimi says.

"Don't you think you have enough files by now?"

"I'm looking for a *particular* file," Mimi says.

"Whose?" I ask.

But she doesn't answer.

"Hellooooo?" I sing, trying to get her attention.

"I'm busy," she says, at the back of the room now. She opens a closet door and discovers a couple of boxes, both filled with what appears to be old files.

"What are files doing in an art room?" I ask.

Mimi shrugs. "In case you haven't noticed, this place isn't exactly what you'd call *organized*."

"But at least this stuff can get us some booty."

"You and your freakin' booty."

"Like it?" I point my butt in her direction.

I think I catch a glimpse of a smile, but then she looks down at the files.

"Let me help you," I say, squatting beside her. "What's the girl's name?"

"What girl?"

"The one with the journal. Isn't that whose file you're looking for?"

"Here," Mimi says. "Check it out for yourself." She pulls the journal from her bag and tosses it in my direction.

Instead of arguing, I flip it open and read one of the entries:

December 3, 1981

I got sent to packs yesterday. It was the first time, but Vicky tells me there will be plenty more. I'm tempted to tell on her. The other night she came to work drunk. She just sat at the nurses' station the entire time, slurring her words as she talked on the phone, calling all her old boyfriends and yelling at them for breaking up with her.

It made me laugh.

The thing is, she caught me laughing and ordered me to go to packs. It was beyond horrible. I wasn't allowed to eat in the morning—not that that's a huge sacrifice. They've been serving leftovers lately, just tossing the slop on tables, making us paw for it like animals. I think some of the cooks are as screwed up as the patients. There's this one cook who used to be a patient here. He likes to show us the scar on his head. He says it's from a lobotomy. The guy's about thirty at most, so I know he's lying. They stopped doing lobotomies here more than forty years ago—at least that's what Vicky tells us. She also tells us that it's too bad they stopped, that some of us could really use one.

Anyway, back to packs. They put me on a table, held me down, and wrapped me up in ice-cold sheets. I couldn't move. I was all bound up like in a casket, and the smell—this strong soap-made me gag. The chill punctured right through my bones and made me want to die. I could hear patients screaming all the way down the hall, making me scream too. They normally only send really disturbed patients to packs, but they also do it as punishment.

I hate Vicky. I'm tempted to tell on her, but I'm scared no one will believe me. I'm also scared she'll make me sleep next to Martha again, that woman who murdered her husband. You have to count your blessings in this place.

Becky's a blessing. We've gotten to be like sisters. She lets me hold her doll, the one she named Christy, after me. I never thought I'd be playing dolls again, but sometimes it helps to pass the time. And sometimes it's kind of fun. I've made one out of tissue, even giving it tissue hair. I've named my doll Rebecca, after Becky.

The other day Becky's dad brought her a big box of chocolates, and she shared some with me. I think

her dad wants her out of here soon, so I'm not sure
how much longer she'll stay. I wish she'd stay as long
as me.

But I just feel like I'm getting worse, like I might
never leave.

I met with Doctor Naslar again, and he upped my
medication.

More medication.

I didn't tell him, but yesterday I could hear
my grandfather talking to me in my head. He was
warning me not to trust Doctor Naslar, that Naslar is
out to get me—even more than Vicky.

Tonight's another full moon. Everyone is wailing.

Including me.

More tomorrow.

"Freaky, huh?" Mimi says as soon as I close up the journal. It appears as that she's done picking through the boxes
of files. She's just sitting there, back on her heels, watching me read—waiting for my response.

"Everything in this place is freaky," I say.

"Do you believe in ghosts?"

"I never used to, but who knows?"

"*I* know," she says. "And they do exist . . . because this
place is full of them."

"How do you know for sure?"

"It's hard to explain," she says, her eyes extra wide. "I
mean, I've always just sort of believed in them. But now

it's different. It's more than just a belief. Something really weird happened after the whole hydrotherapy room thing. I mean, I don't know if it was the room itself. Maybe it's the more I get into Christine Belle's journal. But it's like, I can feel it . . . I can feel *them*."

"Sounds kinky."

"I'm serious," she bites.

"I know," I whisper, suddenly feeling as though there's somebody else in the room, listening in. "So did you have any luck?" I gesture to the files.

Mimi shakes her head and lets out a sigh. "The file I'm looking for isn't here."

"Whose is it?" I ask again.

"My grandmother's," she says finally. "She was a patient here."

"Seriously?"

"Seriously." She nods. "She wasn't crazy or anything like that. She was an alcoholic, and my mother and uncle couldn't take it anymore. Apparently my grandmother would get the shakes all the time. She couldn't hold a job, couldn't take care of herself. She could barely get out of bed sober. I guess it totally took over her life."

I nod, thinking about my dad, about how he shakes a lot, too.

"I mean, I'm not making excuses for them," Mimi continues. "They never should have left her here. Or, since they did, they never should have forgotten about her."

"Did she get better, at least?"

"I don't know," Mimi says. "Because she died here. That's why I was hoping I could find her file. I thought that maybe I could get to know her a little since she died before I was born. I was thinking that maybe I could find her grave marker number—the one they used to bury her . . . since they didn't use names."

"And what if you don't find this stuff?"

"Honestly?" Mimi shrugs. "I don't know. I went to Town Hall and got a copy of her death certificate. But all it said was that she died and was buried here. It didn't say where, exactly. And the lady at the desk told me the hospital didn't keep good records of where people were buried."

"Does your family know you've been doing all this?"

Mimi shrugs. "I've made hints. But it's like they don't want to talk about it too much, not even my older sister, Micki."

"Wow," I say, just taking it in.

"What?"

I suck in my lips, half tempted to tell her about my dad, about how he's an alcoholic, too. I want to tell her that he's the one who gave me my black eye, but instead I grab a folder, suddenly eager for something to laugh about.

"What are you doing?" Mimi asks.

A grin wiggles up my face, just imagining what might be inside—tales of some guy who ingested checkers or something. I open up the folder, and a necklace drops

146

out—this big gold-plated medallion on a chain. "Was Elvis here?" I ask, checking the thing out. The medallion is light in weight, with a pyramid engraved on one side and a monkey on the other, almost like a fake gold coin.

"What's a necklace doing in a folder?" Mimi asks.

I shake my head and slip it on around my neck. "Thank you. Thank you very much," I say, doing my best Elvis impersonation, lip snarl and all.

"Why do you do that?" she asks. "Why do you always have to make everything funny?"

"What do you mean?" I say, holding myself back from playing the air guitar.

"I mean, we should probably get back to the others."

I nod, wishing I could take the moment back. But it's definitely too late. Mimi mutters something about not feeling too well and then gets up and heads for the door.

"Wait." I stand up too.

She lets out a sigh and turns back to face me. "What?"

"I know something that can make you feel a whole lot better."

"I doubt it."

"Actually," I continue, "I know something that can make us *both* feel pretty good."

At first I think she's going to sock me one—give a shiner to my other eye—but then the corners of her lips turn slightly upward, like she wants to know more.

"Come on," I say, holding out my hand. "What have you got to lose?"

DERIK

"THEY WERE ONLY SUPPOSED to be gone a couple minutes," I say, standing up from the circle of candles. I look toward where Mimi and Chet were sitting, noticing that their bags are gone.

Tony gets up as well, chalking something onto his director's clapper, muttering about how we need to get more footage.

I ignore him and pull the walkie-talkie from my bag, resisting the urge to lose my temper completely— especially since Liza's here. "Where are you guys?" I say, pressing the TALK button down.

It takes a few seconds, but then I hear Chet's voice spit out through the receiver: "Hello, Derik," he says, the words all distorted with static.

"Where are you?" I demand in the nicest tone I can muster. "We've got more shooting to do."

"Hello, Derik," he repeats. His voice has a screwed-up

calmness to it, like he's trying to freak me out.

"Don't screw with me, man," I say. "Where *are* you guys?"

"Stay away," he whispers.

"Excuse me?"

"Stay away."

I feel my face scrunch up, wondering what the hell is going on.

"Is Mimi with you?" Greta asks into her walkie-talkie.

"Mimi's on the floor," Chet answers.

"Put her on!" I demand.

"She's on the floor," he repeats.

"You better not be joking," I say. "Is she all right?"

But he doesn't answer.

"Chet?" I shout.

"Stay away," his voice whispers again.

"Tell me where you are," I demand.

Meanwhile, Liza is pacing back and forth, chewing at her thumbnail, totally wigging herself out.

A moment later, a whining sound plays through the walkie-talkie, making me almost drop the thing.

"Chet?" I ask.

"We're in the cafeteria," he whispers. "And Mimi's on the floor."

"Oh my God." Liza covers over her mouth.

"Come on," I say, taking Liza's hand. "Let's go."

We move down the center hallway and into the cafeteria.

"Getting warmer," Chet's voice says through the receiver, obviously hearing the sound of our footsteps. His voice is followed by laughter—a twisted giggle that practically makes me piss myself.

I stop for a second in the center of the cafeteria when I think I hear something—a scuffling sound. "Chet?"

"Getting colder," his voice continues.

"The guy's totally screwing with us," I say, working my way back across the corroded tile floor.

"He's behaving like a spoiled little B-rat." Greta sighs.

"What's a B-rat?" I ask, giving Liza's hand a squeeze.

"A B-rated actor," Tony explains. "They always have to have all the attention."

"Imagine that," I say, somewhat under my breath.

"Getting warm again," Chet says.

We reach the back of the cafeteria, following Chet's voice as he guides us warmer and warmer, until all his cues stop—just out of nowhere.

"Chet!" I call, taking the door that leads out into a back hallway. There are doors to the left and right.

"What happened?" Tony asks. "Did the walkie-talkie go dead again?"

I shake my head, noticing how the ON button is still lit.

"Mimi!" Greta calls. She presses the walkie-talkie right up to her lips. "Are you there?"

But Mimi still doesn't answer.

I reposition my camera so that it rests high on top

of my shoulder and move to the door on the left.

"It's too late to stay away now," Chet hisses, his voice crackling out through the speaker. "I gave you a chance, but now Mimi's bleeding."

"Don't screw around!" I shout. "Where is she?"

"On the floor." Chet's voice giggles, barely able to get the words out. "She's bleeding pretty bad."

"He's delirious," Tony says.

"Where's Mimi?" I demand.

More giggling—like he *is* delirious, like he's completely lost his mind.

"The guy's just being a dick," I say.

"How do you know?" Liza asks, practically welded to my side.

A second later, I hear Mimi scream—a knifelike sound that cuts right through me. "Mimi!" I shout, pulling away from Liza to bust through the door.

But then Liza screams too. She's pointing straight ahead, right at Chet. He's standing by the tunnel, just waiting for us—like some messed-up mental patient.

"Holy shit," I breathe, feeling my heart pump something fierce, noticing the sick-ass grin across his face.

Blood trickles down from his hand. "Mimi's bleeding," he repeats.

"Oh my God!" Liza shrills. She turns away and starts crying—starts pacing around in a circle.

"What happened?" Tony asks.

"What happened is that Chet's jokes suck," I say,

trying to assure myself that this is indeed one of his stupid pranks.

Chet's holding a giant piece of glass. He smiles wider when we see it, like he's seriously enjoying this twisted shit.

"Where's Mimi?" I ask.

At that, Chet passes out. His eyes flutter open. Blood pools onto the floor around him.

GRETA

CHET IS AN absolute idiot.

And so is Mimi.

The whole thing was a joke—the broken glass in his hand, the bleeding, the giggling, the whole *Stay-away-Mimi's-on-the-floor* garbage.

Garbage.

Have I mentioned how much I absolutely *hate* B-rated actors?

And the truly bizarro part? Mimi was in on it. Yeah, that's right. Little Miss Have-Some-Respect-for-the-Spirits-that-Linger herself.

So. Unbelievably. Lame.

Derik's about to blow. Honestly, if I didn't know better, it'd be like one of those cartoons where the top of the guy's head pops off and flames burst out. He's *that* mad.

"It was just a joke," Chet says, standing up. He wipes the fake blood off his hand with a rag. "I bought this stuff last Halloween. Thought I'd bring it along for the occasion. It looks pretty real, doesn't it?"

"*Such* an idiot," I say.

At the same moment, Mimi opens the hallway door and pokes her head out, proving that she's completely unharmed. "It was *his* idea." She grins. "I don't know why I agreed to it."

"I don't know, either," Derik says, his jaw visibly clenched.

"You're not going to like, kick the shit out of me or anything, are you?" Chet asks, still wiping the faux blood from his hands.

"At least you can use the footage for the Bloopers section of the DVD," Tony offers. "But next time, I'd recommend using corn syrup for the blood rather than that ketchupy substance. It's more authentic looking on film."

"A good point," Chet says. "About the whole bloopers thing, I mean. We could sandwich the scene right between the commentary section and the making-the-movie extras."

"You're an asshole," Derik barks.

"Come on, man." Chet holds his bloody hand out for a shake. "Let's make up and be friends." He tilts his head and makes a frowny face, still having fun with this.

"You're an asshole," Derik repeats.

"Lay off," Mimi says. "It was my fault, too."

"We just got a little bored upstairs," Chet continues. "We wanted to go exploring, and you guys seemed a little intense up there."

"Did you not hear me when I said that we should stick together?" Derik asks. He balls his hand into a fist by his side.

"Did you see Tony and Greta?" Chet asks. "They were sticking together enough for all of us."

"It was just a joke," Mimi reminds us. "You don't have to get your panties all in a wedge."

"It was a *stupid* joke," I say, working myself into the drama. I stand "center stage," angling my left profile toward the camera, since it shows off my burlesque mole. "Some of us are trying to make a quality film, here. We don't need a bunch of wannabes screwing it up."

"Touché," Tony says, trying to steal my thunder. He grabs my hand and pulls me away from the camera just so he can take my place.

"Bug off," I snap, completely peeved with his lack of dramatic timing.

"Let's go," Derik says.

"Not until you check *this* room out." Mimi nods toward the door she came out of.

Derik follows her in, making sure to film the sign printed on the door: ART THERAPY. I end up following along too, trying to work my way back in front of the camera. Only, once we get inside, Derik turns the other way, filming some majorly lame-o cow mural—all peeling now. I let out a sigh, tired of having to fight for the scenes I get. It's just like what happens in drama class. Even though I'm the most qualified, Mr. Duncan will almost always pick someone else to play the lead roles. He says I try too hard and that's my downfall. But frankly, I'm sick of trying at all. Even whiney, pathetic Liza gets more camera time than me. *What*, do I need to blubber all over the place? Will *that* get me noticed? I shoot her my most creepified look— squinty eyes and biting teeth—to spook her out. But it only makes her suck up to Derik more. The girl is total casting-couch material.

"I read online somewhere that they used to make the patients do art as part of their therapy," Derik explains, moving to the other side of the room to film more acrylic-paint hell—like patient artwork is more interesting than a live-action scene.

"What do you think of filming a scene with *me* creating something?" I ask. "We could simulate what it was like to work in here; I could act like I'm making a collage."

"Maybe later," Derik says, all but ignoring me—no different, I suppose, than Mr. Duncan himself.

I'm so glad I agreed to be a part of this stellar indie film. *Not!*

DERIK

MY JAW SHAKES. And so does the camera. I take a deep breath to get a steady grip. And pull myself together.

"Derik, what is it?" Liza asks.

Some of the others ask me stuff, too. But I can't really answer. I mean, how do you even put it into words?

I zoom in on the series of pictures, somehow still glued to the wall. They're done in a mix of paint and crayon—a patient chained to a bed; a lady dancing with this huge-ass smile across her face, despite the shock treatment tabs stuck to her forehead; a bunch of patients carrying a casket out to the cemetery; a little boy sitting in a hydrotherapy tub, his teddy bear resting atop the canvas cover; a naked patient crouched in the corner of a stark and empty room; a girl caught in a spiderweb made of barbed-wire spikes.

And a woman with the freakiest eyes I've ever seen. She doesn't have a mouth—just those eyes, and a long, pointed nose. When I zoom in closer to capture those eyes, I notice it—the number seventeen sitting there in place of the pupil.

"Are you okay?" Liza asks. She puts her hand on my shoulder.

I nod, trying to take it all in—all these drawings and what they mean.

"They're amazing, aren't they?" she continues. "Like snapshots of the past—of what it was like to live here."

I nod, taking a second look at the casket drawing, remembering how I read somewhere that sometimes they made the patients build caskets and make grave markers as part of their therapy.

"You getting soft on us, man?" Chet asks.

I clear my throat and shake my head, still trying to get a grip, remembering how they sometimes made the patients bury the caskets, too. Only sometimes the caskets were buried too shallow and got washed down the hill in the rain.

"Jackpot," Chet says, trying to peel one of the pictures off the wall—the one with the barbed-wire web.

"Lay off!" I shout, even surprising myself. I look at Liza to see if I've scared her. I think I have. Her lips are parted and her eyes are wide. "I'm sorry," I say, taking a step back, trying to keep my cool. "But we can't just take this stuff."

"What's wrong?" Mimi asks.

"I just don't want anybody to sell this stuff, okay?"

"How about the works in progress?" Chet asks. He points to the unfinished paintings still sitting on their easels.

"None of it," I snap. "I don't want anybody taking or selling any of the stuff they find in this hospital—are we clear?"

"Okay. Why? What's going on?" Mimi asks, her voice all soft, like maybe I'm the one who's crazy now.

"Yeah," Chet says. "What's the big deal?"

"The big deal is that it isn't ours."

"Well, it isn't theirs anymore either," Chet says. "This place is going to be leveled next week. It's just going to be a pile of trash then."

"So let it," I say. "That's not up to us."

"It's not up to you either. I don't have parents who buy me a brand-new truck every year. I could use the cash." Chet tugs a bit harder on the picture and ends up ripping off a corner.

"Don't be an asshole," I say, taking a step toward him.

Mimi gives Chet a pointed look, and he backs away from the picture—from what he's already done. "This sucks," he says.

"Thanks," I say, unclenching my teeth, feeling myself calm down a bit.

"Drrrrrrama Queen," Greta says, lamely trying to cough out the words.

"Sorry I didn't bring my Oscar," Tony whispers, like I can't hear him.

But I could care less what they think. Maybe I just need some air. Or maybe this place is really starting to get to me. I mean, it's just so weird. At first you don't really notice it too much—walking over the patient files just strewn all over the floor; seeing barred-up windows and scratches on the walls from restraints. And the way this place was just left: trays stacked up in the cafeteria still waiting to get collected; an unfinished game of Scrabble left on a rec room table; a book on somebody's nightstand, the bookmark still wedged inside.

And all this unfinished artwork.

I mean, after a while it just kind of hits you—that these people were real, that they really lived here. And you can't help but wonder what's happened to them now . . . to these people whose histories are being treated like useless shit now.

It makes me wonder if treating people like useless shit became the norm here.

I stare back at the artwork—at those eyes—almost unable to look away. I mean, as cheese ball as it sounds, the art really shows what they felt like—a number, a prisoner, a slave, a headcase.

It only makes me want to make this movie, to get it shown, all the more.

Regardless of whether or not I win the contest.

MIMI

AFTER OUR VISIT TO the art therapy room, we head back to the reception room to decide our next move. The candles still glowing, we sit in a circle on the floor, waiting for Derik to change his camera battery and check out some footage. While Greta tidies up her gigantic cosmetics-case-might-as-well-be-a-suitcase (and Tony assists her), Liza sneaks Christine Belle's journal while she *thinks* I'm not looking, and Chet and I end up sharing a bag of peanut butter–filled pretzels.

"I really want to check out the J-wing," Derik says, replacing the old camera battery for a charged one. "I made up some storyboards for footage over there."

"I take it it's totally haunted?" Greta says with an eye roll.

"You got it," Derik says, scanning through some footage. I lean over to look, catching a glimpse of the exterior of this place—all the pointed roofs and steeples, wings that jet out on both sides like some giant flying insect, and the creepiest water tower I've ever seen. It's this tall bullet-gray tank with antennas that spout out from the top.

"And what kind of pleasures await us in the J-wing?" Greta continues. "More uplifting artwork? Or perhaps something a little bit cheerier—like shock equipment or leftover morgue supplies, maybe? Or better yet, how about some body harnesses between friends? Or another hydrotherapy tub, perhaps? Liza, are you getting all this?"

"Huh?" Liza asks, looking up from the journal.

"Ash, are you feeling okay?" Tony mumbles. He puts his hand on Greta's shoulder.

"My name is *Greta*," she snaps.

"Your name is *Ashley*," he corrects, trying to keep his voice low.

"Are you kidding?" My mouth drops open, mid-chew.

"So what?" Greta shrugs. "Maybe I was born Ashley, but lots of great actors change their names for the stage. Hence the term *stage name*."

"That's so pathetic," I say.

"No it isn't." Liza looks up from the journal. "I know firsthand what it's like to want to change your name."

"You do?" Derik pauses from footage-checking to point his camera at her.

Liza nods. "My parents named me Elizabeth Blackwell. . . . After the first American female doctor?"

"Oh, right," I say, vaguely recalling the name,

remembering something I might have been forced to read in history class.

"So it's sort of like a curse," Liza says. "Having a name like that. It's like my whole future was planned out before I was even born. It's like people have all these expectations of me as soon as they hear my name."

"For me it's the other way around," I say, offering her the bag of pretzels. "People look at me—at the way I dress, the color of my hair, at what I have on for jewelry—and they have expectations, too. I don't even have to tell them my name. I don't even have to open my mouth."

Liza nods, giving me the once-over.

"I mean, let's be honest," I continue. "If it wasn't for this project, there's no way we'd all be hanging out together like this."

"Why not?" Chet asks.

"Oh, please," I say. "Like any one of you would ever be caught dead hanging out with me. I mean, what did you guys even think when you first saw me?"

"Ax murderer," Chet admits, raising his hand to answer.

"Exactly." I sit back on my heels with a sigh.

"But I like ax murderers," he continues.

"I thought you were playing a role," Greta says, darkening in her mole with an eyeliner pencil. "I mean, I guess I assume that of everybody. We're all just actors in one way or another."

"What's with your voice?" Chet asks her, noticing the

change in tone. It's been doing that all night, actually. One minute her voice is all high and whiney, and the next it's this deep and throaty rasp.

Tony laughs in response. "Greta likes to channel her inner Garbo."

"Her inner *what?*" Derik makes a face.

"Greta Garbo," Greta explains, rolling her eyes. "Just about the most talented, the most beautiful, the most prolific Hollywood actress who ever walked the planet."

"Never heard of her," Mimi says.

Greta lets out a sigh and begins the explanation: "Born in Stockholm, Sweden, in 1905, daughter of Anna and Karl Gustafson; started her career in silent film but then transitioned to sound; engaged once, but it fell through; starred in *Mata Hari*, not to mention *Anna Karenina*, *The Kiss*, *The Mysterious Lady*—"

"Greta really digs her," Tony says, like we need the clarification.

"Hence the name change," Liza says.

"So you're a fan," I say. "Big deal. I mean, just because you really like someone's work doesn't mean you have to take their name and try and make your voice sound like theirs."

"That's just it," Tony says, surprisingly eager to dish on his mack mate. "It's not just the name and voice. It's her hair, her style, her mannerisms." He nods toward Greta's beret.

Greta grabs her mammoth-sized powder puff and tosses it at his face.

"Oh, come on, sweet cheeks," Tony whines, unaffected by the powder in his eyes. "You know I'm your biggest fan."

"Well, get in line," she says. "Because Jimmy's a fan, too."

"*Who?*"

"Jimmy Zeplin," she explains. "The phone call I got in the tunnel earlier. He's been begging me to play Mrs. Warble in his off-off-Broadway show."

"You got a callback?"

"And you didn't," she bites.

"I don't know why you can't just be yourself," I say, interrupting their banter.

"Why don't *you?*" she zings me back.

"I *am* myself. I like the way I dress. I don't care what people think of me."

"Not at all?" Chet asks, his face falling slightly.

"Maybe what you like is negative attention," Greta continues before I can answer. "I mean, if I knew people were having all these preconceived ideas about me just based on how I look, I'd try my best to change it."

"Maybe what people should do is not judge others based on appearances in the first place." Tony takes a pretzel and pops it into his mouth.

I nod, noting his squeaky voice, zeroing in on his huge mass of curly brown hair, and knowing for sure that people must give him crap all the time.

"Some people have nothing better to do than judge

others," Derik says, getting this all on film.

"And some people deserve the judgments they get." I eyeball him.

"What's that supposed to mean?" He looks up from the camera.

"Derik *LaPlaya* LaPointe?" I say, feeling my eyebrows arch.

Derik looks at Liza, watching for a reaction. But instead of giving one, she looks away, avoiding eye contact. And so I can't help but wonder if she already knows.

"I'm not like that anymore," Derik says, still looking at Liza, the camera angled toward the top of her head.

"Since when?" Greta asks.

"Since he set his eye on a brainiac?" I say, unable to resist.

"Let's just say I've done some things I'm not proud of," Derik says.

"You're a legend!" Chet cheers. But then the cheer melts into a frown when he notices that nobody else is cheering along with him.

"Maybe we should talk about something else," I say.

"No." Liza closes the journal. "I want to hear it."

"In my own defense," Derik says, trying to make light of it, "except for this one time, I never misled anybody. I never did anything with a girl who didn't understand up front that I wasn't looking for anything serious."

"Except for this one time?" Liza asks.

Derik nods. "This one girl wanted more than I was

interested in giving. I knew that. But I hooked up with her anyway."

"Kelly Pickerel," I say. After the incident, it was pretty much broadcast news around the school, mainly because Kelly was pretty popular herself. But after it happened, she got branded a slut. I can't remember a time when I'd go into a bathroom stall at school and not see her name scribbled across the wall, labeling her a whore, a bitch, a skank.

"*Wow*, she's hot," Chet blurts, ever clueless.

Derik shrugs. "I actually wanted her to be part of this thing . . . so we could patch things up, move on."

"Hold up," Chet says. "You can't tell me that a reputation like yours doesn't have its benefits. I mean, girls like the notorious *bad boy*; everybody knows that."

"Some girls do," I say.

"Yeah, and some girls look at guys like me as only good for one thing—the dreaded 'friend,' someone they can tell all their problems to, the buffer before they go running to guys like Derik. I'm telling you, man," Chet says to Derik. "You've got it made."

"Then how come I feel like I'm losing out?" Derik says. "No matter what you think, it's a lot to have to live up to."

"And that girl you were talking about," Liza begins, "you led her on?"

"It's not something I'm proud of," Derik repeats. "And it's really awkward now, because I see her all the time in school. I know how hurt she was about it afterward. And I know how pissed she still is."

"So here's a thought," I say. "Why not *apologize?*"

Derik shakes his head and then buries it in his hands, enabling Tony to nab the camera and point it at him.

"I don't know," Derik says finally.

"Pride," Tony chirps, still filming. "A guy has pride. He doesn't like to admit his mistakes."

"Yeah, but a real man does," Greta says.

"I'm sorry for laughing at your Greta Garbo ways," Tony purrs.

"I'm sorry for not telling you about my callback," she purrs back.

"Just promise that when I make it big as a director, you'll be my leading lady—like Grace Kelly was for Alfred Hitchcock . . . like Uma Thurman is for Quentin Tarantino."

"Forever, sexy."

Tony returns the camera to Derik, and he and Greta end up in yet another obnoxious make-up fest.

"I probably *should* tell Kelly I'm sorry," Derik says, continuing to film.

"I'm all about fresh starts," I say.

"Speaking of fresh starts," Chet pipes up. "Does this mean you're no longer pissed at me for my little joke?"

Derik smiles, glad for the tension relief. "No," he says. "I'm no longer pissed. So long as you let me frisk you on the way out."

"Switching teams, are we?" Chet asks. "Hate to break this to you, but I'm as straight as a pool stick. And as long as one, too."

"Oh, really?" I perk.

"I'm serious," Derik continues. "I meant it when I said that I don't want you taking anything from this place. That goes for everybody." He glances at Christine Belle's journal.

"How is it any different from what *you're* doing?" Chet asks, sucking the peanut butter filling from one of the pretzels. "Breaking in here and taking footage for your own purposes . . . Don't you plan to make money off this movie? Didn't you say something about RTV and becoming the next hot Hollywood *thang*?"

"Maybe it started out that way," Derik says. "But now I have my own reasons for making this movie."

"And what are they?" Liza asks.

"It's not about *me* anymore," Derik says. "It's about *them*."

"Who?" I ask.

"The people who lived here. I need to tell their story."

"My grandmother lived here," I venture.

"Seriously?" Derik and Liza say in unison.

I nod, telling them how she was an alcoholic, how she was left here by my family, and then forgotten. And how she died here.

"Is that why you wanted to come tonight?" Derik asks.

I nod. "I wanted to find some piece of her here."

169

"Like an ear or a thumb?" Chet asks. "Maybe we should head over to the morgue?"

"Yuck." I push him. "I mean a piece of her memory—some shred of evidence that her last years didn't suck."

"And have you?" Derik asks.

I shake my head and look away. "I mean, I knew the chances were slim, but I still wanted to try."

"How old were you when she got checked in?" Liza asks.

"I wasn't even born yet—wasn't even a thought in my parents' minds. But it happened just after my sister Micki's fourth birthday. Apparently, Micki had this Cookie Monster-themed party, and all her friends were there. After she had unwrapped all the presents, my grandmother dismissed herself to go to the bathroom and then came out without any pants or underwear on."

"Just a granny patch?" Chet asks, grimacing.

I nod. "She was so drunk that she forgot to put her clothes back on after she was done. My mother checked her in after that."

I glance back at Chet, half expecting him to make another joke, but instead his face gets all serious—his lips rolled in and his eyes focused downward.

"What's with you?" I ask.

He shakes his head, staring down at his hands.

"Then how come you look about as happy as a granny patch," I joke.

He shrugs.

"Come on, man," Derik pushes.

More shrugging from Chet, and so I'm half thinking this is all an act—just another one of his stupid jokes. But then when he finally *does* look up, his eyes are serious—sort of a faraway stare that tells me this is no joke, that he does mean business.

"Chet?" I scooch in closer to him and rest a hand on his back.

"My dad's an alcoholic," he says.

"Seriously?" Derik asks.

He nods. "It's how I got my black eye. It's why I'm even here tonight."

"You're here because your father's an alcoholic?" Liza asks.

"It beats hanging out at home with a pissed-off drunk, believe me."

I continue to pat his back, noticing how sad he looks—for the first time tonight—and knowing somehow that it's why he's always making jokes. "Does he want to get help?" I ask.

"Sure. He'll take a ride to the liquor store any time you want to give him one. You can even treat him to some Crown Royal."

"Have you ever thought about having an intervention?" I ask. "I mean, what does your mom think?"

"She got sick of the bullshit and left."

"That's really rough," Derik says.

"I'm sorry," I say, holding back from offering any more

advice—for now, anyway—even though I feel like I have so much to say. After I learned about what happened to my grandmother, I did all this research on how to plan and execute a successful intervention, imagining how things could have been done differently.

"I'm sorry, too," Liza says.

I move my hand down to squeeze Chet's palm, suddenly feeling the urge to tell a joke. Suddenly realizing how much he and I really do have in common.

DERIK

I WANT TO CHECK out some more of my footage. We've been here for several hours, and so I'm thinking I've got some pretty decent shit, but I can't really concentrate.

Liza's just sitting there reading that journal Mimi found, avoiding eye contact. Or maybe I'm being paranoid.

"Anything good?" I ask, bumping her shoulder lightly against mine.

"Yeah," Mimi says. "You've been hoarding that thing for the past hour. Hand it over."

Liza does and Mimi takes the thing, opens it up to the middle, and is just about to read aloud one of the entries when Greta interrupts her: "Do I smell a monologue?"

"What are you talking about?" Mimi asks.

"Let *me* read it," Greta says.

"Why?" Mimi's face twists up.

"Let her," I say, inserting a new tape into the camera. "I think she'll do a good job."

"She'll do an *amazing* job," Tony corrects.

Greta takes the journal and positions herself cross-legged on the floor right in front of me. I hit the RECORD button, and she breaks into the role right away. She reads in a high-pitched voice that sends chills down the back of my neck:

February 20, 1982

I can't stop shaking inside—it's like my blood has morphed from liquid to mush, like it's crawling around inside my veins, looking for a way out.

Becky is gone. Her father came and got her.

And now I have no one.

And so I just want to do it. I've been trying to think up ways. I think the doctor knows, because he upped my meds again. I think he wants to make me crazy, to keep me here forever. He wants to make me his experiment. Everybody tells me it's true, including my grandfather. He keeps talking to me inside my head, telling me how I'll be here forever, how all the doctors and nurses think so, and how Vicky is out to get me.

Now that Becky's gone, I can't trust anyone here.

The nurses are working with the doctor—they're all conspiring to make me crazy. I think they're the ones who put my grandfather in my head. I just want to get him out. I don't want to hear his voice anymore.

At least Becky let me keep Christy, her doll, before

her father took her away. Christy talks to me, too. She has a voice like Julie's, my first foster mom, the one who died—the only one who loved me.

I want to join her in Heaven.

Soon, I think. I will.

C.B.

P.S. I've written a little lullaby for Christy. I like to sing it to her before bed. Rock-a-bye Christy on Witches' Hill. When the wind blows the patients will kill. When the nurse comes, I'll pretend I'm asleep, then shoot her with needles so she won't make a peep.

Greta drops the journal to her lap, and we're all just staring, sort of taken aback by what she read, by how she made it sound.

"That was brilliant, baby," Tony tells her.

"More like disturbed," I say.

"What?" Chet asks. "Didn't your mommy used to sing that little ditty to you?"

"Well, it would certainly explain a lot if *your* mommy sang it to *you*," Greta says, turning to Chet.

"You did a really good job," Mimi tells Greta, getting to the point. "The voice was really fitting—not overdone, you know? Sort of delicate, like how I'd imagine Christine might sound."

"You think?" Greta smiles.

"Totally authentic, babycakes," Tony says. "No faking necessary."

"No faking anything with you." She growls.

"Wait," Liza says, turning to me. "Didn't you say before that you saw a doll hanging from a noose?"

I nod. "The one with the recorder."

"Do you think it's the same one?"

"Negative," Mimi says, before I can answer. "Christine's doll is cloth and her eyes were inked on with fine-point markers when the originals fell out. Derik, didn't you say the one you saw was rubber with those freaky doll eyes that open and shut?"

I nod.

"It sounds like she's really going to do it," Chet cuts in. "To kill herself."

"That's why I haven't been able to read the end," Mimi says. "I almost don't want to know what happens to her."

"Well, I do." Chet breaks open another Yoo-hoo. "Let's hear it."

"No," Mimi says. "I'm not ready yet."

"Well, either get ready or block your ears," Greta says. "Because I have to know." She flips to the last entry in the journal and reads, her voice even more like a little girl's than before—a mix of softness and giggles that seriously creeps me out.

March 4th, 1982

I love my doll Christy. She sleeps with me in bed. Grampy sleeps with me, too. He tells me I'm ready. So does the moth that flies by my bed. I jump on my bed. I fly through the sky. I eat fresh grass. I play on the swings.

I know a way out.

Tonight. After everyone's asleep.

Please, God, don't make it hurt. Take care of Christy. God tells me to hide Christy someplace safe, so they don't take her after I'm gone. Everyone wants to take her. I know they'll take her. I know they'll give her the needle and put her to sleep and take her clothes and feed her mush. I'm sorry, Christy. I'll always love you, but I can't take you with me. I have to hide you someplace safe now. In the auditorium. Under my chair tonight. Number seventeen. At the performance. I'll make sure I get that one. I'll fight for it. And bite for it. And go to packs or a seclusion room for it. I don't care.

I'm going to hide this journal, too. I'll wrap it up in wax paper. If somebody nice finds it, please find Christy. Please take care of her and give her a home.

And help me rest in peace.

> Love,
> Christine

Greta finishes off with an evil little giggle that literally makes the hairs on my arms stand up. "Screw Greta Garbo," Mimi says. "You should be thinking Linda Blair."

"Who?" Liza asks.

"The Exorcist," Tony explains. "The original 1973

version, not the remake. Linda also starred in *Exorcist II, the Heretic*, and she's now the host of *The Scariest Places on Earth*."

"Don't forget that she starred in *Stranger in Our House, Hell Night*, and that film where she plays the teenage alcoholic," Greta adds.

"*Sarah T*," Tony confirms. "Not that I'm some big Linda Blair cultie or anything. I just make it my business to know this stuff."

"Of course," Liza says, with an eye roll that makes me laugh.

"Wait," Chet interrupts, following with a Yoo-hoo belch. "What the hell is up with that journal entry? She can't just end her journal like *that*?"

"Is it just me," I ask, "or are you guys missing the weirdest piece of that whole entry?"

"What are you talking about?" Mimi asks.

"The number seventeen," I answer, aiming my camera at her. "It's everywhere in this place. The graffiti angels going up the wall by the stairs, the patient artwork in the art therapy room—"

"The tombstone someone drew in the A wing," Chet adds.

"And now the chair," Mimi whispers.

"Isn't Christine seventeen, too?" Liza asks.

Mimi nods. "We need to look for the doll."

"And what'll that prove?" Chet asks. "We still won't know what happened to her."

"Yes we will," Liza says. "If the doll's there, then she did it—she killed herself."

"Right," Mimi says. "And if it's gone, she didn't."

"How do you figure that?" I ask, still filming.

"Because let's just say, for the sake of argument, that she tried to off herself but then failed or had second thoughts," Mimi explains. "She would have gone back to retrieve the doll. I mean, just listen to her: the doll is her only friend. She can't live without it."

"Right," Chet says. "But maybe somebody else found the doll. I mean, how many people have broken in here over the years? What are the chances that it's still actually under chair seventeen?"

"Let's go check it out," I say, grabbing the map. "The auditorium is right upstairs."

LIZA

INSTEAD OF TAKING THE stairwell by the cafeteria, Derik says he wants to explore a bit of the male wings. And so we move in that direction, despite all the debris in our path. It appears that pieces of the ceiling have collapsed to the floor, making me more than a little nervous about what awaits us upstairs. Derik's in the lead as we move farther down the G-wing, but he slows his pace every few steps so I can keep up. I think he wants to keep me close to him.

The thing is, I'm not really sure how I feel about that.

Prior to coming here tonight, I *had* heard little snippets about the infamous Derik *LaPlaya* LaPointe. How could I not have? I mean, I may not be Ms. Sally Social at school, but I do have ears.

And I've heard.

Like that time when I was in the bathroom at school and there was this blond girl crying, saying that Derik LaPointe totally broke her heart. She didn't even know who I was, but she warned me to stay away from him, calling him a pimp, a liar, and not even worth the effort of her spit—she actually said that.

The time before that, it was second period of the day and Derik got paged down to the principal's office. The entire junior class was abuzz, saying that the reason he got suspended was because he'd ornamented his locker door with a pair of girl's lacy underwear.

I hated him for that. I didn't even know him, but I hated him, especially since hearing all this stuff sort of ruptured the romantic mystery-boy image that I had built up of him inside my head—after that day, freshman year, by the bus circle.

But now, here I am, totally *not hating* him—totally feeling something, like one of those stupid girls that Chet was talking about, the kind that goes after jerks. I mean, it goes without saying that I had no intention of falling for him. Because, the truth is, I'm *not* like those girls; I don't go after "bad boys." I don't go after anyone, for that matter. I don't have time. And I'm certainly not one of those girls who likes the challenge of trying to transform the "bad boy" into the "nice guy." I'm *way* smarter than that.

And I'm not here to make friends.

So how come these people feel more like my friends than those I've known my entire life?

How come I don't even seem to care about Harvard now?

And why does becoming a doctor seem nowhere near

as exciting as getting to the bottom of this whole Christine Belle mystery?

Or having Derik hold my hand again?

The thing is, he's been nothing but nice to me this entire night, putting my needs way above his own, almost forfeiting his dreams just so I could feel safe.

And for some inexplicable reason that I can't figure out with any equation or look up in any book, I do feel safe with him—even safe enough to stay here, despite all the weird vibes I've been getting from this place; despite how random my behavior has been since I got here.

And despite all the jitters that have been stirring up my insides.

We climb to the top of a stairwell and move down the hallway, our headlights paving through the blackness. This part of the building is beyond dangerous. There are entire sections of flooring that have lost all their ground support, that have caved in on the level below. I keep moving forward, trying my best to watch my step, following Derik's lead as he warns us over and over and *over* again how we need to be careful.

His camera propped up on his shoulder, still filming our every move, he passes the map to Tony and then reaches back to take my hand and lead me over a pile of debris. I ignore it, but then see him grab for my hand anyway.

A moment later, I hear it. A quaking beneath my feet—like the entire floor is erupting.

I scream. My stomach bounds up into my throat.

"Holy shit," Chet yells out.

Before I can dodge it, I've fallen through the floor—one hand barely holding on to Derik's grip, the other clenched on to a thin, rotted piece of floorboard. I feel my fingers slip through Derik's as the weight of my body tugs me downward—deeper through the hole. I struggle to gain a better grip of the floorboard, feeling a jagged piece stab right into my ribs. The more I move, the more the floor crumbles around me, making the hole bigger. I can hear the loose concrete pieces collapse to the floor below.

"Just hold on," Derik says, struggling to get a better grip of my hand. Lying on the ground, he instructs Chet and the others to anchor him in place—to hold his legs from behind so he doesn't fall through as well.

"Hurry!" I shout. My arms shake. The skin over my ribs singes. And the muscles in my fingers are growing weaker by the moment. I turn my head to look down, to see how far it would be to fall. At the same moment, my hand loses its grasp of the floorboard, and I'm just dangling from Derik's grip.

"Look up!" Derik shouts at me.

I crane my head to look back at him. His eyes are wide and urgent like he's just as scared as I am.

"Stay focused right here," he says, blinking. In a fairly stable position now, he grabs both my wrists. He pulls me forward, but the ground crumbles even more, and I scream. Derik slips waist-deep into the hole, but the others pull him back, and he regains positioning.

"Keep focused!" he shouts. "You're not gonna fall."

"Yes I am," I whimper, tears streaming from my eyes. My fingers slip a little farther from his grasp.

"What if I go downstairs," Tony offers. "I could try and catch her."

Derik is panting, trying to gain a better grip. And his hand is bleeding. There's a gash in his palm where he must have cut it.

"Two of you go," he says. Using his forearms, he lifts me upward instead of forward. His face is red and strained. The veins in his neck are protruded. He gets me up just high enough so that I can work my knee onto a solid piece of flooring, while the other knee collapses through the floor.

Still, I feel myself pulled forward, against Derik's chest. He rolls me over against his body, like tumbling from a fire, until we reach stable ground.

"Are you all right?" he says once we've stopped.

I nod, noticing how he's still gripping my hand, hoping that he never lets go.

LIZA

DERIK HOLDS ME AGAINST him for several moments, his face only inches from mine. "Are you sure you're okay?" he asks. His breath is warm against my cheek.

I nod for a second time, staring right into him—at the clenched set of his jaw and that penetrating stare. His pale blue eyes are wide and urgent, concerned for my safety. It's a look that makes me feel all off balance, and so I pull myself closer against him, able to feel his heart beating against mine.

"Say something," he whispers.

"Thank you," I whisper back.

"Anytime." The corners of his lips turn upward in a crooked smile.

"Here," Chet says, breaking the moment. He tosses a rag at Derik's head. Apparently Derik cut his hand on a jagged piece of tile.

"Thanks, man," Derik says to him. "I couldn't have done it without you."

I turn away fast so I don't have to see the blood.

"Are you okay?" Derik asks me, wrapping up his hand.

I nod and tell him about my blood hang-up, that I'm prone to fainting upon even the first glimpse of a trickle.

"It's a good thing you're gonna be a doctor," he jokes.

But I'm not laughing. Because it's true. Because maybe becoming a doctor isn't the right thing for me.

"That was intense," Chet says, still huffing and puffing. He gives Derik's shoulder a high five, and then prattles on about how it was hard to keep Derik's legs down, how he almost lost his grip when the floor collapsed the second time, and how he didn't appreciate Derik's boot heel wedged into his cheek.

Meanwhile, I take a seat against the wall, suddenly noticing how my side is aching. I rub it with my palm and focus on the hole in the floor. It's huge—bigger than the size of a manhole.

"Do you want some water?" Mimi pulls a bottle from her bag and offers it to me.

I take it, still breathing hard, and scrunch myself even farther against the wall, fearing that somehow I might fall through the floor again at any moment. I brush the concrete dust off my coat and glance up at Derik.

He's staring right at me, making me almost lose my breath—again. The smile across his lips widens, like he knows what I'm thinking—what I'm feeling—like maybe he feels it too.

"Hello?" calls a whining voice.

"Tony," Mimi says with an eye roll.

Derik moves cautiously across the tile to peek through the hole. Tony and Greta are standing right under it. Derik tells them to come back up and, once they do, after a few minutes spent catching their breath, Mimi complains that we're wasting time, that we need to keep going.

"We need to find Christine's doll," she insists.

"Are you okay to keep going?" Derik asks, turning to me.

I nod and take Derik's hand as he helps me up—beyond excited when he doesn't let go.

We begin again down the hallway, toward the auditorium. This part of the building is even more dangerous. I mean, corroded floors aside, there are entire patches of ceiling in our path, where the floor above has caved in completely.

Derik aims his camera upward, through one of the open ceiling sections, trying to get his hand to work despite the cumbersome bandage. You can see all the way through—at least two stories up.

I let go of Derik's hand and step away so he can get the shot.

"There's something moving up there," he whispers, zooming in closer.

A second later, pieces fall toward him from above. I go to pull him out of the way, but a couple pelt against his head, and he drops the camera. "Holy shit!" he yells out.

The remainder of the pieces fall at our feet. "Are you okay?" I ask.

Derik nods, rubbing at his head, though he appears to be just fine.

"Holy rocks," Chet says, standing at my side. He kicks the rocks that fell—a pile of palm-sized stones.

"Why the hell are rocks falling from the sky?" Greta asks.

"Not the sky," Tony corrects. "The ceiling."

"Do you think there's someone up there?" Greta asks.

I aim my flashlight beam upward through the hole. It appears that most of the floors above have completely corroded over, making it impossible to walk on them.

"Coincidence, maybe," Derik says.

"No coincidence," Mimi snaps, stooping down closer to look. "There are seventeen rocks."

"Seriously?" I ask.

She nods. "It's Christine . . . I just know it. It's like she's watching us. She knows we're here."

"Does she know I'm wearing SpongeBob boxers?" Chet asks.

Derik shakes his head and lets out a sigh, refusing to buy into Mimi's ideas.

Even though I know she's right.

"I found the auditorium," Tony says, clutching the map. He gestures to a door just a few yards away.

Derik takes my hand again. "Are you ready?" he asks.

I nod. "Let's go."

CHET

INSTEAD OF GETTING a move on, Derik insists that he needs to check out his camera, and so we find ourselves a secure spot right outside the auditorium.

"Is everything okay?" Liza asks him.

"Seems to be," he says, going through all the controls. "I'm lucky."

"Lucky that we haven't bailed yet," Greta adds. "While you're checking your camera, let's check out some footage. I want to see how I look in this pathetic lighting." She readjusts her headlight.

"Are you kidding?" I joke. "We're in the dark. You couldn't look better."

I even catch Tony smiling.

I thought I'd feel weird after telling everybody about my dad's lust for liquor—I don't even know why I did; it just sort of happened—but luckily everything seems pretty cool, especially since no one's treating me any differently. Not two minutes after I told them, Greta pushed me out of the way—literally—so Derik could get a side angle shot of her applying a fresh coat of lip gloss.

So. Not. Hot.

"Check this out," Derik says. He scoots forward on the floor, giving in to Greta's not-so-subtle request to view some footage. He sets the camera down in front of him but angled upward so we can see the screen.

We squat down to look. It's footage from the tunnel—the scene he shot with Greta, Liza, and Tony, while Mimi and I were upstairs.

"What's with all the circle things?" Greta asks, squinting hard to look.

There's a bunch of white globes floating midair, one strategically placed over Greta's butt as she moves down the length of the tunnel.

"They're ghosts," Mimi says. "I saw it on one of those ghost hunter shows. Digital equipment can pick up all sorts of stuff—stuff that isn't visible or audible to the human eye or ear. They call it white noise."

"Seriously?" I ask, noticing how the circles vary in size—much like hooters.

Mimi leans forward to turn up the volume on the camera. "Just listen," she says.

We're forced to sit through an entire cheesy scene starring Derik and Liza as the happy couple gazes longingly into each other's eyes, a candle positioned between them, and tons of asbestos hanging off the corroded tunnel walls behind them.

Now, if that doesn't spell romance I don't know what does.

"Horny little devils," I say, referring to the ghosts. There are a couple of white circles smack-dab over Liza's chest.

Liza folds her arms in response, noticing the globes as well.

"Do you hear that?" Mimi asks.

"I hear Derik trying to hit on Liza," I say, though still taking note of some of his one-liners.

"No," Mimi squawks. "*Under* their voices. Do you hear that whistling sound?"

"I don't hear anything." Derik goes to turn the volume down, embarrassed by his game, but Mimi intercepts him and turns the volume up full blast.

And that's when I hear something—a soft whistling sound, like running your finger over the rim of a glass.

"What the hell is that?" Derik asks.

When the scene ends, the whistling fades into a crackling sound, and you can hear Derik and the others freaking out in the tunnel—just after the door shuts and locks and they can't find their way out.

I lean in closer, feeling a prickling sensation at the back of my neck, noticing how the crackling almost sounds like a voice. But still, it's hard to tell. It's sort of like trying to watch the nudie channel when your folks don't splurge for cable, when all you can hear are a couple of faint ohhh's and ahhh's amid all that pain-in-the-ass static.

"Do you hear that?" Mimi asks. "Someone's talking."

"If you seriously hear talking," Derik says, "then maybe you need to check yourself in."

"Listen!" she barks.

"*I* hear it," I say, to make her feel better.

"You do?" she perks.

I shake my head, since I honestly don't. I mean, aside from a couple of hisses and sputters, I can't make anything out. I lean forward, practically pressing my ear up against the speaker.

Finally I hear something more. It sounds like someone's whispering. "I hear it too," I say.

"Can you tell what they're saying?" Mimi asks.

I shake my head, straining harder to hear, but it's just static again, followed by more crackling.

"Try advancing it," Mimi insists.

Derik does, then pushes PLAY, but it's just silent now.

"Try again," she says.

We spend the next fifteen minutes or so searching backward and forward through footage, listening for more white noise.

Until we find some.

There's a whispering sound in the scene where we first broke in. I close my eyes so I'm not distracted by the action and try my best to concentrate—to focus on the rhythm of the words.

"It's hard to tell," Mimi says, "but it almost sounds like someone's angry. You can tell by the cut of the words."

"What words?" Derik asks. "You can't even tell what she's saying."

"But that's just it," Mimi continues. "You can definitely tell it's a *she*."

I nod, noting that the whispering sound does have a high-pitched quality. "What if it's just radio frequency?"

"I think it's Christine," Mimi says. "Do you hear that? She's singing to her doll." At that, Mimi starts humming out the tune of *Rock-a-bye Baby* right along with the whispering—like some bizarro duet.

"No offense," Greta says, "but there's a shock treatment table with your name all over it."

"Sounds kinda hot," I say. "Is there room for two? I'll even let you strap me in." I give Mimi the sexy-eye, complete with raised eyebrows and pouted lips.

"Wait," Liza says, before Mimi can respond to my invitation. "I hear it too."

"You hear *singing*?" I ask.

But Liza doesn't answer and so I'm assuming Mimi's imagination has gone a little overboard.

But still, there's something there. The whispering is almost clear—the words almost recognizable.

"I've been waiting for you!" Mimi blurts. "Did you hear that? Just like the sign in the hydrotherapy room."

"It sounded more to me like 'Chet is a stud!'" I say.

Mimi rolls her eyes, choosing to ignore me. "It's

Christine," she insists. "I know it is. She's been waiting for me. She needs me to help her. And I'm not leaving here until I do."

Greta links arms with Tony. "As if this evening couldn't get any more insane."

Still, it beats staying home and hanging out with a drunk, especially since Mimi's here.

DERIK

THE AUDITORIUM IS HUGE—like, crazy big. I have to walk a few yards before my headlight beam even reaches the walls. They're completely covered with graffiti—a mix of gang scrawling and stuff like angels and nooses.

Chet lets out a howl, his voice echoing off the ceiling, like this is one big party. While he and the others check things out, I move toward the center of the auditorium, disappointed that Liza doesn't come with me.

It's completely freezing in here. A chill rushes down my back, and breath smokes out of my mouth. I stop for just a second and look around, noticing how I can't see the others now. My headlight beam only shines forward about eight feet or so. But even suckier is that now I don't *hear* anything, either. "Hello?" I call out.

No one answers.

I grab my walkie-talkie, but the piece of crap won't turn on, and so I keep moving, the camera propped on my shoulder.

Until I feel myself freeze.

When I notice the chairs.

They're all set up in rows—at least two hundred of them—as though a performance might start at any second.

The idea of it sends another chill down my back.

I walk toward the first row, the adrenaline pumping hard through my veins, wondering if maybe the chairs are nailed down and that's why they're so well placed. I mean, it's not *just* that the chairs are arranged in rows that's messing me up. It's that they're arranged in *perfect* rows. Like, there's one chair perfectly positioned behind another, and then another, and then another—like someone recently set them up.

I get it all on tape, moving around to zoom in at every angle, noticing the symmetry from every side.

It completely weirds me out.

Breathing hard, I reach out to touch one. At the same moment, my headlight goes out. "Shit!" I shout, standing in complete darkness now. I place my camera down and whack my headlight a bunch of times, but it doesn't work. "Piece of crap!" I shout, going for the flashlight inside my bag. I fumble with the zipper, but I can't get my fingers to work right, especially with the bandage on my hand.

I go to rip it off, but then I hear footsteps move toward me. "Derik?" whispers a voice.

"Who's there?" I call out.

"It's me . . . Chet," the voice says, coming from somewhere behind me. "Are you okay?"

But it doesn't sound like Chet. I whirl around just as a flashlight beam shines in my face—in my eyes—making it impossible to see.

"Derik?" the voice whispers again.

The footsteps continue toward me.

"Are you okay, man?" the voice says.

My face begins to bead up in sweat. My heart pumps even harder. I grab one of the chairs, prepared to throw it.

But then I see Chet's face.

"What do you think you're doing, man?" he asks, noticing the chair—positioned high above my head now.

My jaw shakes, completely freaked out, fully recognizing his voice now. "I didn't know it was you," I say, realizing how messed up that sounds. I mean, it didn't sound like Chet's voice. Something deep inside me told me that it wasn't him—that it *couldn't* be him.

And that someone was coming after me.

"Where were you guys?" I ask, setting the chair down. "I called you. I couldn't see your lights."

"We were in the corner," Chet says, "behind the barrels. Mimi had me picking through a pile of debris. The things you do for lust."

"Man, this place is screwed up," I say.

"You're just figuring that out now?"

"Are you okay?" Liza asks. Her headlight beam moves toward me. And so do the others'.

"I'm good," I say, when everybody's in full view. "I just had some technical difficulties, I guess." I look at Chet—

to see if he's gonna say something, mention how he almost got a chair thrown in his face—but thankfully, he just keeps silent.

"That's too freaky," Mimi says, noticing the chairs. "I mean, you'd think somebody would have trashed them by now. Or at least knocked them over."

I nod, knowing now that they're not nailed to the ground—that they were recently set up.

"Did you find number seventeen?" she asks.

I shake my head, still freaked out that something wasn't right a few minutes ago. That something was messing with me for sure. Still, I take a deep breath and tell myself that this will all be over soon. I reach into the darkness and take Liza's hand, giving it a good squeeze.

"Let the search begin," I say.

TONY

GRETA'S MAKING ME NERVOUS. Ever since we stepped foot in this auditorium, she hasn't been herself. She hasn't been taking my cues or my directions, and she pulled away from me not once but *twice* when I tried to hold her hand.

I'm not sure if it's something I did. I mean, sometimes you just never know with girls. This one time last November she stopped talking to me altogether. I had no idea why, but I couldn't figure it out on my own:

```
FADE IN:

INTERIOR: BAGEL WORLD-DAY

Two attractive thespians, a male and a
female, 17, sit at the corner booth of
a small bagelry, sipping coffee and
sharing a cinnamon-and-raisin bagel.
```

GRETA, the female, is clearly upset,
doing everything in her power to avoid
TONY, her charming boyfriend. Tony
works hard at trying to figure out what
Greta's problem is.

                    TONY
Was it something I said?

          (Greta shakes her head.)

                    TONY
Was it something I did?

                    GRETA
                 (frustrated)
It's something you *didn't* do.

                    TONY
            (trying to be funny)
I didn't tell you how sexy, talented,
and all-over fabulous you are today?

                    GRETA
Are you trying to piss me off even
more?
                    TONY
Is it because I didn't stick up
for you when Mr. Duncan suggested

TONY

you play Carlita's understudy?

GRETA
(arms folded, getting more irritated)
No, but you should have. Carlita is one of
the most talentless actresses in our class.

TONY
(checking date book)
Did I miss some event? Some mark of
time? Our anniversary or something?

GRETA
(look of death)
I can't even believe you have to
ask. Our first date was on January
nineteenth. We went to Sparky's for
dinner right after rehearsal for *The
King and I.* You're such a jerk for not
remembering.

TONY
I'm sorry.

GRETA
You should be.

CUT TO:

After a good twenty minutes or so spent hitting walls, only irritating my beloved all the more by pointing out flaws that she wasn't even aware of in the first place, she finally caved and told me: One full week before, I had gone to see *Casablanca*, this old black-and-white classic with my sister (also a movie buff), not her; and apparently, unbeknownst to me, Greta had really wanted to go.

I scratch behind my ear and wrack my brain, wondering if maybe I unintentionally excluded her from something within the last ten minutes.

It's got to be *something*.

Because she's definitely not herself.

GRETA

IF MIMI THINKS I'm going to go picking through piles of asbestos-littered asylum trash, she's got another thing coming. I'm just about to tell her this, when we're distracted by Derik. It seems his headlight went out in the center of this godforsaken auditorium. I mean, honestly, is this a gym, an auditorium, or what? I can't even imagine what it must have been like to give a performance here—no stadium seating, a constant echo due to excessively high ceilings, and a wooden floor with lines all over it for basketball and such.

"We need to find the chair," Mimi announces like we need yet *another* reminder. Chair number seventeen is all she's been talking about since I read that last entry in Christine Belle's journal.

Though I'll have to admit, asbestos-littered trash and pathetic auditoriums aside, it did feel pretty damned good to read that entry—both entries, actually. Especially since

I sort of got right into the role. I mean, I didn't have to force anything, or fake anything, or improvise one tiny bit. The scenes just sort of felt right—the words Christine wrote, the voice I gave her, my facial expressions, and where I chose to give dramatic pause.

It makes me wonder if that's what Mr. Duncan is always talking about—how I don't get into the heads of my characters enough; I need to trust my instincts more; realize that every role is unique, and that I have to adapt accordingly.

So while the group searches all the chairs, I bite my tongue and try and get into the role as best I can—pretending like I really *do* care about finding the chair, trying to imagine this as one big play and that I'm Christine's ghost, rising above the scene, watching over the others in anticipation as they finally find the doll and give rest to my spirit.

The only problem—there's got to be at least three hundred chairs in this god awful place. And they're *wooden*, for that matter—*the absolute worst!* I mean, I could go into a whole soliloquy on why wooden folding chairs are inappropriate for performance seating, what with their hard backs and lame-o support—but that's a whole other topic.

Right now I need to forget all that. I need to *be* Christine.

I take a deep breath and do my best to be patient. I wander through the aisles as Mimi and the others search the backs and bottoms of chairs. It seems each one has a number written on the back in black permanent marker. But, oddly enough, while the chairs are lined up in perfectly straight rows as though a performance might begin as soon as the curtain's drawn, the numbers are not in order. The front row, for example, goes 29, 85, 108, 217, and so on.

Mimi searches voraciously, like a crack addict who needs her fix. I mean, honestly, Halle Berry in *Losing Isaiah* had nothing on her. Mimi's turning over chairs, inspecting every little crevice, despite what number the chair is. While she and Chet work one side of the seating area, Derik, Liza, and Tony work the other.

Until it appears they're all done.

"I checked all these out," Chet says, after what feels like a good half hour. He motions to the rows behind him. "I can't find seventeen."

"Are you checking under all the chairs anyway?" Mimi asks.

"Well, yeah," he says, his eyebrows weaving together since it's pretty obvious he's been checking *everywhere*. He's been picking up and turning over chairs right in front of her. Everybody has.

"We're done, too," Derik says.

"We're *not* done," Mimi argues. "I mean, we can't give up now."

"Nobody says we're giving up," Chet says.

"Nobody?" Tony lets out a sigh.

"We have to keep looking," Mimi continues. "Christine

is counting on us." Without waiting for backup, she moves toward the stage area. I can see the lovely heap of debris from here.

I take a deep breath and concentrate on my "inner Christine," trying to channel her character and get inside her head. "We need to help her," I say finally.

Tony's mouth drops open in response, and I almost lose my concentration. Still, he joins us as we climb the steps to center stage, where there's another complete mess—torn theater curtains, piles of trash, a dust-covered stretcher, a stack of moldy magazines from the Seventies, a container of blue things (a pair of blue Barbie shoes, a child's blue toothbrush, a blue hair comb, blue bottle caps, a thimble of blue thread, a plastic blue frog).

And then a clown costume. One of those polka-dotted ones with the big frilly collars.

"To go with the mask," Chet says, holding the costume up like he wants to try it on.

The whole scene makes me sad, not because of the clown, or the mess, or Tony's sulky attitude. But because of Mimi.

She really wants to help Christine.

And deep down, I feel somehow that Christine really wants to be helped.

"Are you okay?" Liza asks, noticing that I'm not myself.

I give a slight nod, pausing a moment, center-stage, to look out at the rows of chairs, wondering what it might have been like to perform here.

"Do you want some water?" she continues.

I shake my head and move back down into the audience.

"Where are you going?" Tony asks.

But I don't answer; instead, I choose a seat in the middle row, knowing somehow that that's where Christine would have sat—not so far back that she would have missed the show, but not so close that she would have caused extra attention.

"Greta?" Tony calls.

But still I don't answer.

"Is she okay?" someone asks.

I close my eyes to block them out, pretending to hold a doll in my hand. I prop her up on my knee as though she's watching the show, too. There's a female singer tonight. Draped in layers of light blue silk, she has a tinkling little voice that reminds me of wind chimes.

"Are you ready?" I whisper to my doll.

I imagine that Christy is scared, and that it takes some coaxing to convince her to go under the chair, promising her a world of safety and love, far away from this wretched castle. I tell her that when she's found, her new mommy will take good care of her, and that one day she too will be able to wear layers of blue silk, just like the pretty singer tonight.

But Christy doesn't want to go.

She frowns at the roll of tape I've brought along, the one I snuck from the nurse's station, telling me there's no way she'll last under there, that the tape will lose its strength and she'll go tumbling to the floor, that she'll get swept up with a pile of junk, just like everything else in this place.

"Take me with you," she says, though her lips don't move.

"I can't," I say. "I want you to be safe. And I won't be around to take care of you."

"Then leave me someplace else," Christy continues, her sparkly blue eyes, the ones I drew in for her when the others fell out, stare up at me—urgent, full of expectation, and fearful all at once.

Just like me.

"Greta?" says a voice, followed by a hand on my knee.

It completely startles me, completely takes me out of the moment. I look down at my lap to see if the doll is still there. But it's just Tony. He's kneeling down in front of me like something's desperately wrong.

Derik and Liza are standing a couple feet behind him—Derik getting footage of this entire scene.

"Are you okay?" Tony asks.

"Fine," I say, hearing the defensive tone of my voice, checking around the aisle to see if maybe I dropped the doll.

"Well, you were sort of mumbling to yourself down here," he continues. "We've been trying to get your attention for the past ten minutes. I had to get my clapper." He flashes me his director's clapboard.

"I'm fine," I repeat, my head fuzzing over.

"Are you sure?" Tony remains unconvinced.

I nod, knowing that I hadn't heard them trying to get my attention; that I must have been so sucked into the moment, trying to channel Christine and get inside her head, I completely blocked them out. I tell myself that it must have been like one of those weird dreams you have—the kind where you wake up so abruptly you think that what you dreamed was actually real.

Why else would I continue to look around for the doll on the floor?

I shrug, confused by it all—and a little scared. I mean, nothing like this has ever happened to me before. For at least ten minutes I really believed it—I really believed that I was Christine, that I was talking to her doll, and that my one and only wish was for Christy to be safe.

After I'm not around.

"This place is screwed up," Derik says. "It messes with your head."

Liza nods. "I haven't been myself since I got here."

"I'm okay." I stand, finally feeling like I've gotten a grip.

"So what happened?" Tony asks, still looking for an explanation.

"The doll isn't under the chair," I tell him.

"What do you mean?" Liza asks.

"I mean, Christine knew better than to stick the doll under a chair. She cared too much about her."

"What are you talking about?" Derik asks.

"Just listen," I say, holding the ache in my head. "Can't

you hear me? Christine was *going* to hide the doll under a chair; she had the whole thing planned out. She even stole the tape. But she couldn't go through with it. She knew the doll wouldn't be safe under a chair."

"Holy shit," Derik whispers.

"How do you know all this?" Liza asks, taking a step closer to me.

"What difference does it make?" I snap.

"Wait, the doll isn't here?" Mimi moves toward me.

I roll my eyes, more irritated by the moment, not wanting to get into the whole explanation all over again—especially since it seems so unexplainable.

My neck itches. My head pounds. "I've got to get out of here," I say, suddenly feeling nauseated.

"Are you all right?" Liza asks.

"Keep looking for the chair," I manage, covering my mouth. I hurry away, eager for fresh air. But it's just darkness all around me—a thick perpetual darkness that crawls under my skin and clogs up my throat.

"Where are you going?" somebody shouts after me—Derik, I think.

But I don't look back. Instead, I go for doors, trying each one, looking for some way out.

"Greta!" Tony shouts. He grabs me by the arm and forces me to look at him.

"I have to get out." I cough. "This place is making me sick." I turn away from him to try another door. The knob turns, and suddenly I'm outside.

I breathe in the night air, my lungs filling up with chilly goodness, feeling a little bit better—more myself.

"Holy shit," Derik says, somewhat under his breath.

We're on the roof of one of the buildings. It's a large flat area like a deck where people can walk out, where they can see as far as Boston, a good fifteen miles away.

I gaze up into the sky, noticing how the stars are right above me, how it's actually warmer out here than inside.

"This is so not safe," Mimi says, looking down from the rooftop.

What's weird is that there are no gates—no walls or fencing or framework. No boundaries whatsoever to keep someone from jumping off.

At that moment, I feel my heart stop, somehow knowing the fate of Christine Belle. There isn't a doubt in my mind.

"This is how she did it," I whisper. "She jumped from here."

DERIK

IT'S TIME to go.

I tell everyone this, but Mimi won't hear of it.

"No way," she balks. "Not yet."

"We're going," I insist, aiming my camera out over the rooftops of the other buildings, noticing how it's a good three stories down. "I don't like the shit that's been going on. This place is starting to mess with our heads."

"I agree," Greta says.

"No!" Mimi shouts, moving toward the edge of the rooftop.

"What do you think you're doing?" I ask her.

But she doesn't move. She stares at me with this wicked look—like a girl possessed—like she's silently challenging me to stay. "Not yet," she says, standing only inches from the edge now.

"Maybe we should stay for just a little while longer," Liza offers.

"You *can't* be serious." I turn toward her.

Liza nods, meeting Mimi's eye, like somehow they're on the same wavelength.

"Okay," I cave, agreeing for Mimi's sake, but fully intending to bust out of this shit hole just as soon as we get the chance.

Chet reaches out to take Mimi's hand and lead her from the edge. "What are you trying to do?" he asks her.

But she doesn't answer.

We move back through the rooftop door, into the auditorium.

And that's when we spot it.

There's one of those wooden folding chairs right in our path, just a few feet away. It's folded open, like it's been sitting there waiting for us forever.

"Holy shit," Chet whispers.

"That wasn't there before," Mimi says, stopping dead in her tracks.

"It must have been," Tony argues. "We just didn't notice it, is all."

My heart totally stops, noticing how the seat of the chair faces us, like some messed-up invitation.

"We walked right by here," Mimi says. "I definitely would have noticed it."

Liza nods, snuggling in closer to me.

Still, I tell myself there's some logical explanation: we must have had our heads so far up our ass cracks, trailing around after a half-crazed Greta as she led us out onto the rooftop, we didn't even notice the chair.

I *tell* myself this. But deep down I'm not really sure that I believe it.

Mimi goes over to inspect the thing. She shines her flashlight over the back, and then stops to look up at us. Her eyes are wide. Her mouth trembles open.

I feel myself swallow hard, hoping to God that it isn't the one, that it's just some random chair.

Mimi swivels the chair around so that the back faces us. The number is clear—written in black permanent marker: #17.

MIMI

I FLIP THE CHAIR over in search of the doll. But it isn't here. It isn't wedged up underneath the seat, or balled up in a corner, or wired to one of the legs.

Just like Greta said.

"Where is it?" I ask her.

Greta's lips bunch up like she has no idea what I'm talking about. So I continue to search the legs, like the doll might appear at any moment.

"Give it up," Tony says, butting his big fat hairball head where it doesn't belong.

"Mind your own business," I snap, continuing to pull at the chair.

"She's crazy," he whispers, like I can't hear him.

I pick the chair up and smash it against the floor— anything to get inside the legs.

"Hold up," Chet says, grabbing the chair from me.

"Stay away from me!" I shout.

Instead he tells me to relax, that he just wants to help me. With a bit of straining, he pulls off one of the rubber stoppers, desperately searching every inch of the chair.

But nothing's inside the leg.

He tries for another, but the stopper doesn't come off so easily. He fishes inside his bag, pulls out the knitting needle he found earlier, and uses it to pry off the stopper.

Finally it works. And a rolled-up piece of paper falls out, making my heart clench.

"I think that's for you," Chet whispers.

My hands shake before I can even pick the note up. I unravel it, noticing the yellow moldy color and how the edges are worn with age.

It's from Christine. I recognize her handwriting.

March 4, 1982

Dear Christy's new mommy:

I couldn't leave her here. But rest assured, she's safe. I've hidden her in my room. If you found my journal, you know which room it is. She's hiding in my headboard—in one of the loose posts—waiting for you.

Please take good care of her. God bless!

Sincerely,
Christine Belle

"We need to go back there," I say.

216

"What we need is to get the hell out of here," Derik argues, pointing his stupid camera in my face.

"No!" I shout. "We have to help Christine."

"We will," he says. "This movie is going to be shown. Contest or not, people are going to see what this place was like. I'll make sure of it."

"We need to do more than that," I say. "We need to find the doll."

"Why?" Derek squawks. "What the hell difference does a doll make?"

I look away, not knowing how to explain, but then I just say it: "It's because of my grandmother, okay?"

"What about her?" Derik asks, his face bunched up in confusion. "She was sent here. She died here. It sucks."

"You can be a real asshole, you know that?" Chet says.

"He didn't mean it," Liza argues, trying to make nice for him.

"I'm sorry, all right?" Derik offers. "But I really think we should go."

"We're not going," I say, feeling my jaw tense. "I came here to help my grandmother, and I'm not leaving until I do."

"Wait," Liza says, turning to me. "How is helping Christine going to help your grandmother?"

"It won't." I sigh, knowing that I'm not making much sense. "But maybe it will help me. I came here tonight to find evidence of my grandmother, to get a taste of what it was like for her during her last days here—

since nobody else in my family seems to give a shit."

"And you've done that," Greta says.

"Yes, but I wanted to do *more* than that. I wanted to find her file, but I couldn't. I wanted to find out where she was buried, and I failed there, too. Yet, for some reason, I've found all this stuff about Christine. So maybe I can do some good after all. Maybe I can help someone else rest in peace. I mean, for all I know, maybe my grandmother even knew Christine. They were here at the same time—at least for *some* of the same time."

"I don't like what this place is doing to us," Derik says.

"Ditto." Greta nods.

"I mean, between you on the roof and then beating the shit out of that chair," Derik continues.

"Don't forget *you* a few minutes ago," Chet says. "When your headlight went out."

"Right." Derik nods, refusing to get into it.

"What happened?" Liza asks.

"This place is really messed up," Greta interrupts, looking out into the darkness, toward where the rows of chairs are—where only minutes ago she pretty much lost it too.

"But going back to Christine's room . . . finding the doll . . . it could be really cinematic." Tony taps a finger over his lips in thought.

"I don't know," Derik says, still getting the scene on film.

"Please," I insist. "Then we can leave."

"Count me out." Greta shakes her head and takes a step back.

"I don't know," Liza says. "I mean, part of me thinks that we *should* do this—that it's our responsibility. I mean, we've been here for hours, taking advantage of this place, of all these memories—when we don't even belong, when the memories aren't even ours. It's almost like we owe it to this place—to Christine, at least—to do this."

"Are you kidding me?" Greta balks. "Little Miss I-want-to-go-home-this-place-doesn't-want-us-here? You can't honestly tell me that you don't want to leave."

"No," Liza says, huddling in even closer to Derik. "I do. I mean, I'm scared out of my mind. It's just, it's hard to explain, but it's like, I'll be even more scared if we *don't* do this."

"Exactly," I say.

"What do you think, Chet?" Derik asks, as though suddenly we're voting on it.

Chet shrugs and takes a step closer to me. "I've got nothing better to do."

"Sorry," Derik says after a pause, "but I'm the director of this project and I need to do what's best for everybody. I think we've been here long enough."

"We've worn out our welcome," Greta says in agreement.

Still, I shake my head, silently refusing to leave.

DERIK

IT'S A LITTLE AFTER four a.m., and while I'd planned on staying here all night, I feel like it's time to go.

I just hope I'm doing the right thing.

I give Liza's hand a squeeze, thinking about what she said before—how it'll be even scarier for us if we don't find Christine's doll. But still, I have to do what I feel in my gut is right. And right now what I'm feeling is that we've been here for way too long.

"You don't think I'm a jerk for making us go, do you?" I ask her.

Liza shrugs. "I honestly don't know what the right answer is. Nothing's been clear for me since I stepped foot in this place."

I nod, only slightly reassured. Meanwhile, back in the reception room, Chet sets the knitting needle he found on the floor, ditching his ideas of selling stuff on eBay; while Mimi, Miss Packrat herself, leaves behind all those files

220

she found. Instead she crams only Christine Belle's journal and watercolor picture into her bag, which, all considered, is okay with me.

"Are we ready?" Greta asks.

I give a slight nod, still focusing on Mimi. I mean, it's definitely suspicious—the sheer fact that she's so willing to cave, that she isn't bitching me out and putting up a fight. "What's up with you?" I ask her.

"What do you mean?"

I shake my head, knowing that she's definitely up to something. "Maybe you should stick close to me on our way out," I say.

"Screw you," she says, shutting me out by holding up her hand like some wannabe homegirl.

"I'll keep an eye on her," Chet says, totally glued to her side.

I nod, though I don't fully trust him either. And so, all the way out, I keep looking back, making sure she's still there, that's she's still following along, right beside Chet.

"Don't even think about sneaking off," I tell her, pressing the TALK button down on my walkie-talkie. But, no surprise: the crap box isn't working again.

About ten minutes later, after booting our way through the underground tunnels at a pretty decent clip, Mimi announces that we're in the A wing. Her voice echoes off the walls, cuts through the darkness, and makes my heart jump.

"It's right above us," she shouts.

"That's nice," I yell back, knowing full well what she's thinking—how Christine's room is right upstairs, how it'd be no big deal to just take a quick peek.

"She does have a point," Chet says.

"No chance," I say, focusing on the door up ahead—the one that leads to the tunnel that travels under the hospital grounds—confident that we're doing the right thing, since, for some reason, I have this crazy-ass feeling that if we don't get out now, we never will.

"This is it," Tony says, shining his headlight beam over the map. "We pass through here and make the stretch across. Then we'll get to that outlying building, the one we first entered."

"Right," I say. "And then we can hike back down the hill."

He nods as I wrap my hand around the knob. I go to pull it open, but then I pause to look back. Mimi's gone.

And so is Chet.

I shake my head, holding myself back from shouting out some four-letter words of choice.

"Where'd they go?" Liza asks.

"Where do you think?" Tony says.

"I don't care," Greta says, brushing past me to go for the door. "I'm leaving anyway."

But the door doesn't open.

"It's locked," she says.

"It can't be." Tony steps in to help her. But go figure:

his toddler-size muscles don't do the trick. And so I try as well, kicking at the door, body-shoving it, and doing my best to break the knob right off.

But the thing still won't open.

"That's *it*!" Greta shouts—even pissier than me. She takes off down the tunnel, in the opposite direction of the door, in search of another way out.

"Hold up!" I shout at her. "We can't just go out through any door we want."

"We can't just leave without Mimi," Liza corrects.

"Why can't we?" Greta asks. She turns around to face us. "If Mimi wants to stay here, then let her."

"We're not leaving without her," I say.

"*You're* not," she corrects. "I'm outta here. If you want out too, then follow me."

At that, Greta turns on her heel and starts to run down the tunnel like she's got a rocket shoved up her ass. Tony tries to stop her, but she's ignoring him, too.

"We have to find Mimi," Liza says. "We won't get out of here unless we do."

"What do you mean?"

"I mean, I feel like we made a mistake. We should have told Mimi that we'd stay in the first place. Our business here isn't finished yet."

"What are you talking about?" I say, running my fingers through my hair in frustration.

"I mean, before, earlier . . . when we first got here," Liza continues, "I felt like something about this place didn't want us here. But now it's like it doesn't want us to leave. Not yet."

I take a deep breath, my head spinning with questions—with what to believe. I shake my head, refusing to deal with it. Instead I move down the tunnel toward Greta, readying myself to restrain her if I have to, noticing that Tony's not having any luck. She heads up a set of stairs.

"You're not going anywhere!" I shout.

Liza follows close behind me. I grab Greta by the arm, and she kicks me in the face—hard. Her heel nails me in the jaw, and I stumble back.

Meanwhile, Greta keeps running, Tony trailing after her. I can hear them on the first floor. I move in the direction of their voices, my jaw aching, my heart speeding up.

But I finally spot them. Greta's working the lock of one of the exterior doors, trying to get out.

"You're gonna get your asses arrested," I shout. "As soon as the cops see you hiking across the grounds, you're bagged."

"I don't care," Greta says. "I just want to get out of here." The lock clicks, and she goes to turn the knob.

But it doesn't work.

She pulls out her cell phone and tries to dial. But it's not working either. "Give me your cell," she tells Tony.

He pulls it from his pocket and checks the screen. Apparently it's all out of charge.

"Come on," I tell Greta.

But she ignores me and heads down the other end of the hallway until she finds another door—one that leads to a stairwell that takes you outside.

"No need to run after her," Liza says, holding me back by the arm. "She won't get out. The door will be locked."

"How do you know?"

A second later, Greta starts kicking at the door, slapping her palms up against it, like that'll make the thing open.

"What's going on?" Greta cries out.

Liza shrugs off a chill, completely unsurprised by the door.

"How did you know?" I repeat.

"This place is crazy," Liza whispers.

"We need to get the hell out of here," I say, wrapping my arm around her, knowing for sure that we need to find Mimi. That we need to help Christine.

That it's just like Liza said—our business here isn't finished until we do.

MIMI

DERIK DOESN'T LEAVE me a choice. And so when he isn't looking, I grab Chet, and we duck inside a utility room, switch off our headlights, and hold our breath. It's beyond rancid in here—like mildew mixed with turpentine paint.

Still, when Chet pulls me toward him, farther into the room where it's completely dark and we won't be seen, where the pure blackness blankets over everything else— any fears, any doubts, who we are, and where we're stand- ing—I'm able to bury myself into him. I press my face against his chest, and he wraps his arms around me and pats my back, allowing me to catch my breath.

"It's almost over," he whispers.

I nod and pull him closer, noticing how if I really con- centrate, I can smell the inside of his closet—a caramel scent. His breath is rhythmic—like a metronome that keeps me focused on the moment.

"We need to get going," I say, hearing the others run by.

Our embrace breaks, and we both sort of stand there for several seconds, waiting for the other to move.

I hold my hand up in front of my face, completely unnerved when I can't see my fingers wiggling.

"Chet?" I say, after several moments.

He doesn't answer.

"Chet?" I repeat, a little louder this time. I reach out to feel for him, but he isn't there. My hands swipe through the black and empty space.

A banging sound comes from the corner of the room. "Chet!" I shout, feeling my heart beat fast.

"Get out," a voice whispers from somewhere behind me—a female voice.

"Christine?" I whisper. I go to click my headlight back on, but it doesn't work.

"Get out," the voice repeats, her tone both angry and urgent.

I maneuver as best I can through the darkness, trying to find my way back to the door, accidentally tripping over a bucket of some sort. I hear myself yelp.

"Right here," a voice says. It's followed by a hand on my shoulder, totally making me jump.

I whirl around. At the same moment, Chet clicks his headlight on, so that I can see his face. The light shines in my eyes, forcing me to squint. "What the hell are you doing?" I shout, pushing against his chest.

"Relax," he says, holding me back. "I was just checking things out."

"Were you in the corner?" I ask. "Were you whispering stuff to me—telling me to get out?"

"Not this again." Chet rolls his eyes. "Maybe what you heard was Greta running by."

"No!" I insist.

"What are you saying, you don't trust me? Look, I was only trying to help. I was just making sure the coast was clear."

I take a deep breath and try to decide whether I should believe him.

"It's clear, by the way," Chet continues. "The coast, I mean."

"Fine," I say, trying my headlight again. This time it works. I take a second peek behind me, deep into the utility room, half expecting to find something—*someone*—else. But there's only us. "Let's go," I whisper, and move out into the hallway.

LIZA

THE HOSPITAL IS keeping us captive. I honestly feel that way, as irrational as it sounds. With Chet and Mimi missing, it's just the four of us now. And nobody's really talking.

I grab Derik's hand as he leads me around the spot where the stairs collapsed. "Are you okay?" he asks.

I nod, pulling myself together, relieved somehow that we're doing the right thing.

"It's this way," Tony says, using the map.

The hallway does look familiar. We're in the A wing, searching for Christine Belle's room, since that's obviously where Mimi and Chet sneaked off to.

We move slowly down the length of the hallway, our flashlight beams mingling together, crossing over one another, but then becoming one solid strip of light.

I look to the left, toward the room that I sneaked off to earlier—when I opened up the closet and found a rope tied into a noose, almost like a warning of the horrors yet to come.

Derik wraps his arm around me as we approach Christine's room. The door is open a crack. "Are you ready?" he asks.

I nod and take a step away from him, edging the door open just a little. I can see Mimi from here. She's sitting on the ground, rocking back and forth, Christine's doll cradled in her arms. And she's crying, whimpering like she can't get a grip—like I've never seen her before. I don't even think she notices us as we enter the room.

Nor do I think she cares.

Chet is with her, trying to be supportive. He sits behind her, patting her back, but I'm not sure she notices him either.

Derik locks eyes with him, wondering what to do. I look up for just a second, noticing how the headboard has been taken apart; the cover of one of the posts, about three inches in diameter, is ripped off completely—where Christine hid the doll.

The idea of it—of righting someone's past so far into the future, of helping someone's soul rest a little easier, maybe—gives me chills.

"We should go," Derik says.

Chet nods and helps Mimi up, taking her bag so that she can keep a firm grasp on the doll.

We leave, back down the hallway and down the stairwell, finally coming to the door that leads into the tunnel—the one that gets us out of this place.

"What are the odds that it won't be locked this time?" Derik asks, wrapping his hand around it.

"Pretty good," I whisper.

Derik turns the knob. And this time it works.

"Holy shit," Greta whispers.

She and Tony huddle together, as do Derik and I, and Chet and Mimi. We travel quickly, keeping a good pace until we reach the outlying building—the one we first entered.

Derik pauses at the door, afraid it won't open, maybe. Even though I know it will.

And it does. The outer door opens, too.

"Flashlights off," Derik orders, just before we step outside.

We click them off, in total darkness now, but it doesn't matter. Because we're finally out.

We may never be free of this place, but for now we're out.

ONE MONTH LATER

· · · · ·

LIZA

April 22, 2007

Office of Undergraduate Admissions
Harvard University
86 Brattle Street
Cambridge, MA 02138

Dear Director of Admissions:

Please accept this as a formal letter of deferral for my fall 2007 admission. I would like to defer my admission until the spring semester, at which time I would like to pursue an academic course load consisting of my arts and science requirements, rather than concentrating in chemical and physical biology right from the start, as I had originally planned.

I would also like to take this opportunity to express my enthusiasm about attending Harvard, particularly as an undeclared major. Please be assured that this deferral does not in any way detract from my genuine interest in attending.

To be quite honest, since my initial application to your university, I have grown and learned a lot, really taking the opportunity to ask myself what it is I want to pursue, both academically and professionally.

For the first time in my life, I feel that I am making my own decisions, that life is throwing me a series of tests, and that I owe it to myself to complete these tests, to see what direction they're trying to point me in. I plan to take the fall semester to find out.

Many thanks in advance for your understanding, and for your faith in my academic abilities. I look forward to seeing you in the spring.

Sincerely,

Liza Miller

Liza Miller

· · · · ·

Dear Mom and Dad,

I know you don't understand the choices I'm making, but they are my choices. It's not Derik's fault, so please stop blaming him. He's not the irresponsible person that you make him out to be. He's doing something important with his life, and he makes me happy. He's supportive. He listens to me. And he's always able to make me laugh.

Right now that's what I need. Actually, when I really stop and think about it, I'm not so sure how I lived without these things for so long.

I hope one day you'll understand.

Love Always,
Liza
xoxoxoxox

TWO MONTHS LATER

. . . . .

TONY

ASHLEY'S *THE REAL WORLD* AUDITION TAPE-
PART I OF IV

STARRING
ASHLEY BARBOSA (the actress formally
known as Greta)

DIRECTED BY
TONY CASSIS

ALSO STARRING
"RYAN SEACREST": BILL DRISCOLL

PAPARAZZI: JENNA MATHERS, DONNA
TIMPECK, ALLAN FEINER, JEREMY BLOOM,
DAN RAKOWSKI

A-LISTERS: TIA LAMB, SUZANNE DOWNEY,

JENTI WREN, CASEY RAMOND, JOHN
ROMANOWICZ

PHOTOGRAPHERS: JASON GARBER, HYACINTH
BAILEY, ROGER MING

ASHLEY'S BODYGUARDS: KEVIN KNEELAND,
MARK GREICO

SUMMARY
ASHLEY WALKS "THE RED CARPET" ON OUR
RE-CREATED VERSION OF OSCAR NIGHT.

EXT. KODAK THEATRE-NIGHT

A thick red carpet lines the sidewalks.
Floral arrangements decorate the area.
A-LISTERS take time to pose for PHOTOG-
RAPHERS. Cameras FLASH as people mill
around, schmoozing and getting inter-
viewed. Giant lifesize OSCARS stand in
the background.

PULL BACK to reveal a black stretch limo
as it pulls up to the curb. ASHLEY BAR-
BOSA, 17, emerges from the car. PAPARAZZI
and photographers swarm, but the velvet-
covered roping keeps them at bay, as do
Ashley's two hulky BODYGUARDS.

ASHLEY stops a moment to pose for the photographers. She shows off her gown, a strapless peach-colored satin number that all but reaches the ground. Just her Jimmy Choo heels peep out from the bottom.

"RYAN SEACREST," 30-something, steps forward from a throng of onlookers to interview.

ASHLEY. Meanwhile, cameras continue to FLASH. Paparazzi eavesdrop on their conversation, taking notes.

> RYAN
> Hi, Ashley. You look gorgeous tonight. Can you tell us who you're wearing?

> ASHLEY
> Thanks, Ryan. This is a Vera Wang original.

> RYAN
> Gorgeous. And how are you feeling tonight? I loved *Project 17*, by the way. How does it feel to be a part of the first Best Documentary Short nominee to be shot for under a hundred dollars?

ASHLEY

It feels amazing, Ryan. I'm really
excited about it. Really happy about
the nomination.

RYAN

And you changed your name.

ASHLEY

Right. I can still be a Greta Garbo fan
without trying to clone myself into
her. A good lesson to learn.

RYAN

Any other lessons for aspiring actors?

ASHLEY

Yes, acting isn't about the thinking;
it's all about the feeling. Each role
is unique. And each character needs to
emerge from within. Period.

RYAN

Well, great. Great advice. And we
can see the fruits of that advice
right here, with the film's
nomination.

ASHLEY

That's right, Ryan.

RYAN

So what can your fans expect from you
next?

ASHLEY

I'll be starring in another indie.
It's about an overly emotional drama
queen at an arts high school. We start
production this summer. It's being
filmed by Tony Cassis, an up-and-coming
Boston-based filmmaker.

RYAN

I don't think I've heard of him.

ASHLEY

Well don't worry, because you will. Not
only is Tony amazingly talented, but
he's also quite sexy.

RYAN

I take it, the two of you are pretty close.

ASHLEY
(grinning)
You could say that.
(speaking to camera)

Hi, babycakes. I love you.
  (Ashley blows the camera a kiss.)

                    RYAN
Good luck tonight, Ashley. We look
forward to seeing more of you.

                  ASHLEY
Thanks, Ryan.

CUT TO:

THREE MONTHS LATER

· · · · ·

MIMI

June 1, 10:22 PM, rainy night

Our visit to Danvers State feels like it just
happened yesterday. I know that sounds
clichéd, but clichés aside, I can't seem to shake
the place—can't seem to get it out of my
bones.

The post-traumatic stress stuff still lingers.
I'm having trouble sleeping, and I still jump at
every little noise in the house—from the toaster
oven bell to the creaking of floorboards.

I don't know if the sedatives Dr. Maylor
gave me are helping, but at least I haven't
woken up in the middle of the night this week
screaming Christine's name.

My parents are pretty worried, though. My
mom continues to blame herself for my PTSD.
The other night I heard her talking to my dad,
saying that if only she had been more open with

me about my grandmother, if only she and my uncle had made different choices back then, maybe I wouldn't have felt the need to go to Danvers in the first place.

But my trip to the hospital was never about making anyone feel guilty. And I have no idea why this whole post-traumatic thing even happened. All I can guess is that maybe I wasn't as prepared as I originally thought.

Or maybe that place just makes people crazy.

Regardless, Dr. Maylor says I'm good to go back to school in another week (just in time for finals). He also thinks that all this journaling is actually helping me make progress in my therapy.

Little does he know, however, that keeping this journal only makes me remember Christine more.

Her journal still sits in a duffel bag in the back of my closet, along with Christy, her doll. Dr. Maylor says that one day—sometime when I'm completely healed—I should go back and look at that stuff, just to prove to myself that I'm stronger than that place and those memories. But for now I can't imagine when that time will ever come.

Chet seems to be the only one who understands that. I've grown so much closer to him. He's been visiting me more often lately, usually at night, right after my tutoring sessions.

He keeps me updated on all his dad drama, which helps me focus on something besides shrink-speak and schoolwork and talking about what it is I'm supposedly feeling all the time.

He and his older brother got together last week to confront their dad, and apparently the old man has agreed to get some help for his drinking. It's all still very fresh, so I have no idea what will happen.

All I know for sure is that I love having Chet around.

Last night he came over with a pint of my favorite pistachio ice cream. We ended up camping out on my bed, eating our way to the bottom of the container, and laughing at stupid stuff—like our trig teacher's green polyester suits and Ms. Pimbull's obsession with the Chia Pet. The poor woman has at least eleven of them in the art room, and she calls them her kids.

I was laughing so hard I could barely even swallow my ice cream. And then Chet dug his spoon back into the container and scooped up the very last bit. He held it at my lips, waiting for me to relax—his face all serious, just staring at my mouth. After a couple seconds, he slipped the spoonful over my lips. And then he kissed me, his mouth folding over mine in pure creamy goodness. My heart beat fast and my skin tingled over, like snowflakes swirling all around me.

We continued to kiss some more after that—until well past midnight, when he was supposed to leave.

I can only hope there's more to come.

More soon,
Mimi

SIX MONTHS LATER

· · · · ·

DERIK

A LOT'S GONE DOWN since that night at Danvers State.

First: I didn't win the contest. Not that it really matters, because, hey, at least I tried.

The thing is, something really weird happened after my experience at Danvers State. It may sound kind of cheese-ass, but spending the night there made the problems with my parents seem so small. So I ended up telling them all about the movie after all—even though I didn't win. At first they were cool about it. My dad told me about some guy he knew who had stayed at Danvers State—some guy who thought he was the real Burger King—crown, robe, and all. But then I got to the part where plans had changed for me—that I wasn't going to work in the diner.

And that's when things got ugly.

My mom was ripshit. I mean, beyond—yelling at me in Canuck, telling me I had shit in my head. My dad didn't say much at all, just sort of sat there listening, clenching his granddad's spatula tighter than he holds his rosary beads. That's the part that made it hard—seeing how disappointed he was.

It took a full five weeks to actually convince them to sit down and watch my film. But then, once they did, after it was over, my father got this huge-ass grin on his face, even though he didn't say anything. My mother was happy, too. I know she was. She cut me a slice of blueberry pie and set it in front of me, squirting a giant swirl of whipped cream on the top. For her, that says a lot.

A couple months after I sent my entry in, I got a letter in the mail from RTV—the contest people. It was a personal letter, not one of those standard photocopied ones, telling me that they really liked the project and encouraging me to keep working on the footage and try again.

Which is exactly what I did.

So, in the end, I didn't win the internship, but RTV ended up selecting a handful of student documentaries taken from the submissions pool to air on the show. I guess it's sort of like what they do on *American Idol*—when they show some of the auditions—except RTV actually chose quality student documentaries to air, calling them runners-up. The actual winning entry will be on in a few weeks.

I've named the movie *Project 17*, after the chair, not to mention all the other messed-up references to the number that we encountered that night. It's weird; I can't even look at the number now—on the clock, on the calendar, on a price tag—without thinking about that stupid chair.

The movie airs tonight, and I'm having some people over to watch, including Liza. That's where another one of my changes comes in. She and I are dating. We've been together for six months, ever since the project.

We're setting up the family room since it's got the widescreen, waiting for everybody to arrive. I've loaded up the tables with stuff like cheese pretzels (the organic kind for Liza) and my parent's contribution of celebratory sparkling cider (though I've got the real stuff).

"Are you nervous?" Liza asks, clicking the TV on.

I shake my head, knowing that I probably should be. But I honestly feel like I did good work.

"This is just the beginning for you," she says.

"For both of us," I clarify, stopping a second to really focus on her—on how unbelievably amazing she is.

Her eyes crinkle up like she's just as excited as me. "I'm really proud of you, you know that?" she says, her tone all serious like she really means it.

I really mean it too. I hold her hands. They feel so smooth, like bars of soap. "How did I get so lucky?"

Liza smiles—a wicked little grin that sneaks up her lips, like there's just something secret about her that I have to know.

"You know," I begin, "a very wise person once told me that there are close to three hundred germs living in the human mouth, and that kissing—sharing those germs—can help support the immune system."

She leans in closer. "Care to boost your immunity?"

I nod and press my lips against hers, noticing how she smells like vanilla candles—and how she tastes like tangerines.

When the kiss breaks and we finally come up for air, I click on over to RTV. "Forty-five more minutes," I say, glancing at the clock.

I can hardly wait.